The Red Tiles:

Tales from China

Cao Wenxuan

Translated by Huaicun Zhang

Paths International Ltd

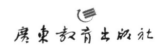
廣東教育出版社

Cao Wenxuan's novel, Pure as Water

"The wind blows the white clouds, and the white clouds scatter in the sky, changing shape constantly. The rolling waves of the sea under the vast sky look like an endless stream of blue silk, thick and soft. The sunshine shimmers through the clouds and the golden rays bounce over the water."

I am often immersed and extremely excited in Cao Wenxuan's words, looking at the world through his water-like prose, feeling time stop, feeling the harmony of all living things. Reading his novels takes me to a special place where his words paint a rainbow of colors cascading from the sky onto lush green trees, where branches and leaves tremble happily together. And where pouring rain suddenly falls from that same colorful sky onto the earth below, creating a beautiful natural symphony; floating, calm and omnipresent.

Cao Wenxuan is a great writer. He writes with passion.

He said: "Reading can't change the starting point of life, but it can change the end of life. Reading can't change the length of life, but it can change the quality of life."

He writes what he believes. His words, whether in novels, prose or picture books, possess a unique and fresh quality that combine the simple, the natural, and the real.

Wenxuan said that in his hometown, from every direction

you can see water. In the rainy season, the river rises and the water appears to be boundless. The villagers live surrounded by water. Stories are told and events take place by the water, in the water, and on the water. Nowadays, although he lives in the city, the village in which he grew up remains forever in his memory. In his book *Reading Is a Religion*, he wrote the following sentence: "Water nourishes my soul and nourishes my words."

In fact, Cao Wenxuan's words also nourish the minds of thousands of readers who love him as much as I do. I have the habit of taking notes while I read. I copy into my notebook all the wonderful sentences and paragraphs that impact me the most. I have done this while reading Cao Wenxuan's novels ever since I was in junior high school and I now have 16 notebooks on my bookshelf. I'm not sure when, but eventually I started to use my paintbrush to describe Cao Wenxuan's words, and I have now produced a dozen books in which each painting is accompanied by written paragraph from his books.

I love Cao Wenxuan's words and all the descriptions of nature and scenery in his novels. This love has been passed down to my daughter Xian. She treasures all his books and keeps them on a special shelf in her study. Once, when she was in the sixth grade of elementary school, I was on a business trip in Beijing. In the afternoon, I went to Tsinghua Universiey with An Wulin to visit Mr. Cao. I remember while we were eating my phone rang. I answered it, and to my surprise all I heard was Xian crying and shouting loudly: "Mom, Bronze is dead! Why did Uncle Cao let Bronze die?" She was only nine years old and happened to be reading *Bronze and Sunflower*. We were anxious about Xian, as well as somewhat amused by her emotion. Cao Wenxuan took the phone from my hand and said: "Xian, Bonze is not dead, Bronze is able to speak." In fact, the first time I read *Bronze and Sunflower*, I cried, too. This is the power of words.

I love reading. I dreamed of the day when I would help produce a set of Mr. Cao's books. It took two years to obtain his transcripts. Editors, Bian Xiaoyan and Dai Miao are also loyal fans of Cao Wenxuan. Their love of Cao Wenxuan's works is no less than my love for Cao Wenxuan. Guangdong Education Publishing House have designated the publication of Cao Wenxuan's novels a key project. They have carefully designed and used Cao Wenxuan's texts in order to select paintings from different famous artists, allowing literature and art to collide beautifully so as to spark the imaginations of children.

Cao Wenxuan's words are philosophical and beautiful, inspired by his hometown, childhood, and dreams. They are like water: pure, transparent, and nourishing. Opening this set of novels, you will embark on a wonderful journey. You will return to the innocence of childhood, to the rainy watery hometown, to the place where you have been to many times in your dreams from which you didn't want to wake ...

The Red Tiles is now available in English to all readers, and this could not have been achieved without my friend Sally and my daughter Xian. In order to best present the pictures and images that Cao Wenxuan described in his stories, Xian and I spent an entire summer in Mr. Cao's hometown in China. As we observed details from the shapes of the houses, to how the river nourishes and sustains the lives of its people from babies to the elderly, we sensed the depth of Mr. Cao's great love for his hometown. My daughter Xian was raised in England, where she grew up reading Mr. Cao's stories. Her understanding of the stories helped me enormously during the translation process. Translating more than 100,000 words from Chinese into English is not easy, especially when trying to present the original story accurately to the reader. This could not have been done without the help of my dear friend Sally, who was born and raised in England and worked in the field of television press and public relations. She proofread and edited the entire book, word by word. We spent countless hours discussing the use of words and language in order to illustrate a particular object or action so that we would paint an authentic picture. I believe readers will love this book from the first moment they pick it up.

Zhang Huaicun

Contents

The Story of Herding the Ducks

The summer holiday was approaching, and two children, Bovini and Magpie, were to go with Grandpa Duck to herd ducks at the reed marshes a dozen miles from the village. Grandpa Duck was over sixty years old, with a swarthy face and a loud voice. Bovini was fat and dumpy, with chubby arms and short legs. He skipped everywhere like a calf, making rat-a-tat sounds with his little feet everywhere he went. Magpie had a big forehead, a smiley mouth, and his little eyes always shone with satisfaction.

Grandpa Duck's eyes narrowed as he grinned with delight whenever he saw the two lovely boys.

One

There were many small fish and shrimps in the reeds, thus the little ducklings were well fed and grew quickly from fist to hand-size. In addition, their yellow fluff was beginning to turn white. Because of this, Grandpa Duck knew he would have to build a bigger fence around the duck yard that day, and so didn't go out to herd the ducks with Bovini and Magpie.

Bovini and Magpie rowed their boat and called out, "Duck, duck."

Brandishing a bamboo pole, they drove the ducks to the place with the most fish and shrimps.

The marsh was extremely beautiful. As the wind from the

south blew, the green reeds huddled together, rustling in the breeze. Waterfowl of all colours fluttered playfully in the water and on the shore. Occasionally, they flew off, chirping happily, up into the sky.

Bovini and Magpie both made hats out of lotus leaves to shade their heads from the sun. Then, they made whistles by rolling up reed leaves and blowing into them with their mouths. They felt an indescribable happiness.

The sun went down in the west, and a vast expanse of fiery sunset radiated brightly over the reeds. Time went by quickly and it was soon close to dusk. The ducks were now full up and nodded off on the grass, lying contentedly with their bills nuzzling down into their feathers.

Bovini said to Magpie, "Keep an eye on the ducks. I'll give the boat a wash and be right back."

Magpie put his hand to his heart and promised, "I will! Everything will be OK!"

Later on, after he had finished washing the boat, Bovini returned. When he counted the ducks he found that a very beautiful speckled one was missing.

He glared at Magpie, "What did you do? Where is the duck?"

Magpie felt so ashamed because he had lost the duck. He went quiet and began to slowly tear a reed whistle apart.

Bovini asked angrily, "Why don't you speak? Have you lost your tongue?"

Magpie threw the broken leaves onto the ground, still without a word.

Bovini stood with his fat arms akimbo, "Oh ... now you're frustrated? What about the lost duck?"

Inside, Magpie knew he was wrong, but he was stubborn and reluctant to admit his mistakes. "Are you Grandpa Duck?"

Bovini was enraged, and his little fist clenched involuntarily. He really wanted to hit Magpie to relieve his anger.

Magpie jumped forward like a fighting cricket, and shouted, "Come on! You just try!" He pressed his chest against Bovini's fist.

Bovini, realising that he had raised his fist, quickly put it down.

Magpie was still shouting, "Come on! Why have you dropped your fist?"

Bovini took a step back.

Magpie pushed his nose towards Bovini's fist, shouting defiantly, "You are as timid as a mouse! Come on! Hit me!"

Bovini puffed out in anger, then gave Magpie a sharp push with both hands. Magpie fell flat on the ground and was so upset that he burst into tears.

"Quack, quack," the little lost duckling that had caused all the trouble came strutting towards them!

Magpie got up, wiped his tears, and waved the bamboo pole wildly to divide the ducks into two groups.

Bovini asked, "What are you doing?"

Magpie wouldn't look at him, and with his hands on his hips, said sullenly: "I won't herd the ducks with you!"

The two children looked at each other defiantly!

The ducks could be divided into two groups, however, the boat couldn't be split in two! Magpie stretched the long bamboo pole with reed flowers hanging under it out of the boat to keep the ducks apart. Then they both took up an oar and began to row. But, Bovini was much stronger than Magpie, and therefore as they rowed the boat, the unevenness of their strength made it sway on the river like a dragon whipping his tail, which frightened the ducks.

Grandpa Duck watched them from a distance ...

Two

Grandpa Duck filled a big basket with duck feces, and then asked the two boys to stand back to back. He took a pole and put one end of it on Bovini's shoulder and the other end on Magpie's.

"Now, carry it away, together, "Grandpa Duck said seriously.

The two boys had always been very competitive, so one of them went to the left and one to the right, which meant neither of them was able to take a single step!

The children were amused, thinking, *Why is Grandpa Duck being so silly! How can we carry something away together when we're standing back to back?*

However, Grandpa Duck again said seriously, "What are you doing? Go! "

Bovini and Magpie looked at Grandpa Duck. They both felt confused.

Grandpa Duck patted their heads and said with a smile,

"Look, if you don't work together, you won't even succeed in carrying away the duck feces. So you two need to cooperate with each other and work as one."

Bovini got angry easily, but was also quick to calm down. Magpie was stubborn, and thought that although he had made a mistake, it wasn't right for Bovini to lose his temper with him.

Grandpa Duck took a basket, gave it to Bovini, and said, "Go to the shallow water to get some snails. Two of the ducks are sick."

"Grandpa, please give me a basket too," pleaded Magpie.

Grandpa Duck poked his forehead and said, "You two must share that one."

On reaching the shallow water, the boys took off their clothes and jumped in. Magpie found some snails and went to the basket that he saw was right next to Bovini. He stopped and thought, *but I haven't made up with him yet.* So, not wanting to put his snails into the basket, he picked a lotus leaf and placed the snails onto it instead.

Bovini, noticing that Magpie hadn't put his snails into the basket, decided to place it between them. Then, they both began throwing snails into it like shooting hoops in a game of basketball.

Bovini wanted to talk to Magpie, but his heart was pounding and he was a little nervous.

When he saw grandpa Duck was looking at him from a distance, he picked up his courage and asked Magpie cautiously, "Are you ... cold?"

At that time, the sun was blazing and the water was warm!

Magpie turned to Bovini and smirked at him, without

5

saying a word.

Bovini wiped the sweat from his face and said, "Are you still angry? Let's make up!"

"Why bother? I lost the duck!"

This annoyed Bovini and he climbed onto the river bank. He threw his clothes over his shoulder and walked away angrily, like a bull that had been whipped. In his frustration, he didn't even seem to be aware of the reeds by the roadside as they brushed against his body.

Magpie felt a little regret as he watched Bovini walk away. A few moments later, he too climbed onto the bank with embarrassment.

Three

In the middle of the night, the herons among the reeds suddenly began to squawk. Grandpa Duck knew that when the herons called out at night it meant there was a good chance that it would rain the following day.

The next morning, Grandpa Duck said to the boys, "It is likely to rain heavily today, so I will stay home and repair the duck yard fence while you two go and herd the ducks."

Bovini and Magpie drove the ducks into the deep reeds. They didn't speak to each other. Bovini was bored, so he started to sing in his squeaky voice. Magpie was singing as well. But as neither of them felt happy or really in the mood for singing, the sound they made was tuneless and out of key! After a while, big black clouds covered the sky and the wind began howling from the northwest. The reeds swayed violently and snapped loudly as some bent and broke. All kinds of birds squawked and screeched and flew to the reeds to take shelter from the wind. Soon the rain poured down from the sky like a shower of scattered beans.

Bovini and Magpie were still not friends!

It was the wind that caused trouble for them this time. A strong gust of wind suddenly swept through the air and made one group of startled ducks flee to the south and one group to the north.

As the saying goes: If ducks are frightened by the rain, no one can catch up with them. These ducks spread their wings and, at lightning speed, ran desperately away.

The wind grew stronger and continued to damage the reeds. And the rain pelted the ground, leaving little holes in the mud. The ducks ran faster, leaving the children behind. If they didn't manage to chase the ducks into the shelter of the reeds, some would get injured, and some would get lost!

The two children were so anxious that they almost cried.

"Stop!" Bovini gasped at the ducks. But how on earth could the ducks understand him! He couldn't count how many times he had fallen over, and he was now covered in mud. Usually as strong as an ox, his legs now felt as heavy as lead and as if they were tied together tightly with rope. He could hardly move.

Magpie wasn't having much luck either. The ducks ignored him and ran away as fast as they could. He was tired and hungry. He yearned to rest, but he knew he must catch the ducks first. Just as he was about to slow down, the ducks suddenly stopped rushing about. He looked up and saw that Grandpa Duck had arrived and was blocking the runaway ducks with a bamboo pole.

Grandpa Duck watched Magpie carefully, but didn't help him immediately. Then after a little while, they both drove the ducks into the reeds, and then helped Bovini.

As Grandpa Duck washed the mud from the faces of the two children, he asked, "Are you two still rivals? "

Magpie said first: "No! I don't want to be! "

Bovini said, "Me neither! We know that was wrong."

Grandpa Duck looked at the two lovely boys, and smiled indulgently ...

Written in August 1975

Modified on September 28, 2013

A Revolt of The Dolls

At the corner of Blue Tile Street, there was a shop that sold dolls.

Hundreds of dolls were piled up in the back warehouse. The warehouse had no windows and half of it was underground, so the dolls lived in complete darkness.

The shop was owned by Mr. Marlin.

The dolls in the warehouse had been rejected by Mr. Marlin over the course of many years. A doll called Big Head had first been thrown into the warehouse seven or eight years ago. One of his arms had been bitten off by a rat the year before last, and his left shoe was missing because that same rat had chewed it off and run away with it.

In the store upstairs, the shelves were all made of the best quality solid wood. Every doll put on these shelves was carefully selected by Mr. Marlin. His shop had been open for many years and it was very famous. Although it was quite busy all year round, during festivals it attracted many more customers. Mr. Marlin was very proud of his store's excellent reputation. He told himself, *I'll never put an ugly doll on any of my shelves! Even if business is so good that all my stock gets sold, I would rather close my door for a while than sell the unattractive dolls I have abandoned in the warehouse.*

As you can tell, he was extremely particular about his selection of dolls.

In the eyes of most people, all the dolls he ordered from

the manufacturers were exquisite. However, there were always several Mr. Marlin was not satisfied with, and he never hesitated in picking them out and throwing them into the warehouse. He could not remember how many rejected dolls he had flung in there over the years.

Actually, there were more than one hundred dolls of all sizes piled up in the warehouse. The dark room was damp all year round, especially in the monsoon season, when the dolls felt uncomfortable in the humid moisture-filled air. The walls were moldy, and so were some of the dolls that had been thrown onto the floor. A musty smell is the most unpleasant odour in the world. Because the door was always tightly closed, the dolls could not breathe freely and often felt suffocated by the stale atmosphere. Sometimes when he left the warehouse, the door didn't close properly behind Mr. Marlin, and the dolls would crowd around the door desperately trying to breathe in some fresh air from the outside. They looked rather like a group of fish that had floated to the surface of toxic waters so they could inhale the clean air of a sultry summer evening. Occasionally, the lovely scent of flowers wafted into their dark room from the outside, and the dolls would close their eyes with pleasure as they became giddy from the beauty of the fragrance. Their bodies would become soft and dizzy and they would almost fall to the ground. If the door wasn't closed properly in July, the scent of lilacs would often drift into the musty dark room like smoke. When this happened, the dolls would breathe in very deeply, wanting to draw the intoxicating fragrance into their souls.

The darkness made them feel depressed and hopeless. It

seemed to have a powerful influence on them.

Time seemed to pass by very slowly in the darkness, like a sluggishly flowing murky river, rather than a steady stream of clear running water. Sometimes, when a gleam of light penetrated the room, they would feel as if they had suddenly come across a fresh and shimmering waterfall during a long walk through a dark wood.

What affected them most was their loneliness. Although there were more than a hundred of them crowded together, they felt so miserable that they seldom spoke to each other. The damp, musty smell and the darkness kept them in a permanent state of depression, and even despair. As the years passed, they were silent most of the time. And in the silence, what they felt most deeply and clearly was loneliness. How bitter they were! And they had no idea where this life would take them, or how it would end.

One afternoon the door opened and Mr. Marlin carelessly tossed in another doll.

It was a tiny doll, smaller than any other doll in the warehouse. As soon as the door opened, it flew through the air like a black shadow straight towards Big Head. He ducked instinctively, but eventually it hit him right in the face. However, Big Head didn't feel any pain, which showed how small and light the new doll was.

The doll, who was known as Tiny, fell to the floor and murmured, "What am I doing here?"

That amused the other dolls, and many of them laughed.

"What's so funny?" asked Tiny, when he looked up and saw all the other dolls. This made the dolls laugh louder.

As they laughed, a doll named Little Butterfly began to cry.

After a while, more dolls began to cry. As the laughter died down, all the dolls were silent except for the ones that were crying. It was an eerie silence, like the desolate wilderness in winter. Tiny didn't understand, and wondered why some of them were crying. After a while, he fell into a restless sleep.

It was late autumn now, and when he awoke, Tiny felt very cold. He wanted to talk to the other dolls, but in the darkness he couldn't see them. He turned his head to look for some light, but couldn't find any ... not even a glimmer. So when he got up to walk around he kept bumping into the dolls, first this one, then that one! As he stumbled into them, they became very annoyed.

"Don't you have eyes? "

"I can't see you! "

"So why are you walking around? Can't you just stay still? "

Tiny was unhappy and thought the dolls were really bad-tempered. He lay on his back on the ground with his legs bent and his hands behind his head. He was angry.

Two blue lights, the size of green peas, suddenly appeared in the corner of the room. Moments later, a few more little lights came into view. At first, the lights were fixed in one place, but soon they began to scatter. When Tiny first saw them he wasn't afraid. Instead, he was excited. At last there was something that lit up the darkness! He smiled at the lights, and felt relieved ... like a small lonely boat adrift in the dark sea would feel when it suddenly spots a lighthouse, or the masthead light of an approaching ship.

He was just about to shout with delight to the other dolls,

"Look! Light! " But all at once he began to tremble. "*It is ... a rat!* " he thought to himself.

"Rats!" he yelled out at last, and jumped up and ran towards the back of the room, knocking over several dolls as he went.

The dolls had been fast asleep. All they could do in the endless darkness was sleep. Tiny's scream woke them up, and they panicked. Some stiffened with fear, and some huddled together in terror.

Little Butterfly was shivering behind Big Head when she saw the blue lights. There were about four or five pairs of lights, but because they were darting about the room, it looked as though there were many more.

Big Head, who had been bitten by rats before, comforted Little Butterfly saying, "Don't be afraid!"

The blue lights moved towards the dolls. Tiny, who was very scared, was standing in front. He tried to turn around and go to the back, but the other dolls were crowded so closely together behind him that it made it impossible for him to get past. All at once, he found his courage and no longer felt afraid. He turned around and faced the rats fearlessly.

When the rats approached him, he shrieked loudly, "Argh!" No one would have imagined that the very smallest of them could have such a mighty and fierce voice. The blue lights suddenly disappeared as the rats scurried into their holes. Still screaming at them, Tiny continued to walk menacingly step by step towards them as they rushed away.

When they saw this, the dolls cheered up. Even Tiny himself hadn't known he could make such a scary noise. As the rats all retreated into their holes, he continued to bellow. The sound of his deafening roars made him feel very strong, and even powerful! He loved this feeling!

13

When everything was calm once more, Tiny said to others,

"There is nothing to fear. If they come out again, we will yell together!"

When the rats came out of their holes again and the blue lights flickered randomly in the dark, at the signal from Tiny, all the dolls shrieked at the top of their voices. The sound was like the roar of wind and thunder. Then as if they'd been extinguished by a hurricane, the blue lights suddenly went out.

As the days went by, Tiny began to understand why he had been left in the dark warehouse. He cried in secret for a long time. When he heard that Big Head had been here for many years, he began to spend his time sleeping, just like the other dolls. When he woke up, he had no idea how many days he had been asleep. He sat up cross-legged on the floor. The sound of snoring surrounded him. He also heard someone crying in their sleep, and he assumed that the sobbing came from Little Butterfly.

Tiny didn't fall asleep again. Day in and day out, he stayed awake. One day, without even knowing what day it was, he stood up. Immediately, he almost fell straight back down again because his legs were numb. He shook himself a few times and finally was able to get to his feet.

He said loudly, "Wake up!"

He couldn't tell if the dolls had heard him or not.

He said in a louder voice, "Wake up! Listen to me!"

He shouted again.

All the dolls woke up.

Tiny said to the dolls, "We need to revolt!"

He was very serious. The dolls were either not fully awake, or were unable to understand what Tiny meant, and they were silent.

"The rats are certain to come again. One day they will understand that our yelling is harmless and can't hurt them. We can't defeat them. They will destroy us and we will die!" Tiny, feeling as strong as a mountain, felt like he was looking down from a great height at all the dolls.

"Let's revolt!" said Tiny, waving his fist in the dark.

By now, all the dolls had woken up, but were subdued, as if they were standing in a cool autumn wind. Although they could not see Tiny in the darkness, they seemed to sense his firm fist waving in the air.

"We will revolt not only because of what the rats might do to us, but also because we are all dolls and we must stand together!"

The other dolls had never thought about this before.

Tiny continued, "We are dolls! We were created to be with an owner, albeit different owner. Maybe a young child, a four- or five-year-old girl, or an elderly grandmother. Maybe someone who lie in a hospital and may soon die. Either way, it is our right and duty to be with someone. Perhaps one of us will travel around the world with their owner, or listen to their owner every night telling the beautiful and moving stories that his mother had told him. Happiness is our right, and no one can take that away from us!"

The dolls listened in silence.

"We need to revolt!" Tiny said firmly.

"Yes! Come on! Let's revolt!" Big Head said.

"Revolt!" said the doll with the long arms who was nicknamed Gibbon.

The dolls sat in excitement in the dark for a while. The shouts of "Revolt" echoed in the darkness.

It was night-time and outside it was dark. The city was a port. The horns of great ships thundered from the sea. The long dull booms could be heard come tremblingly through the darkness and the fog.

There was a doll that wore glasses, who had been in the darkened basement for five years. He was the most talented doll of all. Not only could he write poetry, but he could also compose. The others called him Four Eyes. Most of the time he was silent. He sat alone in a corner, anxious and sad, perhaps because he thought his destiny was to live all his life in this endless darkness. He spent his time writing poems and songs. He rarely made a sound. He just sang and chanted softly in his heart. Sometimes, when he read his verses or sang out loud, all the dolls would listen attentively. They would be deeply touched by his poems and songs, and would weep to the lyrical sounds of his voice.

Now that Tiny had encouraged the dolls to rise up and rebel, Four Eyes began to write both the words and the music for their protest song. After singing it to himself many times, he finally began to sing aloud in the dark:

"Wake up,
Noble dolls!
Rise up,
And fight side by side!
Open the door of darkness,
We must follow the light,
Like moths!

We are behind the door of death,

No escape hatches,

No time to manoeuvre,

Only to fight to the death,

On to the road to freedom.

It is today,

We must bid farewell to the despair of yesterday,

Open your arms to greet tomorrow!

Tomorrow! Tomorrow!

The brilliant tomorrow!

Wake up! Dolls!

Rise up! Dolls!"

All the dolls puffed out their chests with pride as they heard the song.

Tiny said, "Every one of us needs to sing this song! We are going to start our revolt with this song. We will put the past behind us!"

But the big question was, how to open the door?

Big Head said, "Based on my observations over the years, the lock is between one and a half meters high. But the tallest of us is less than one meter. We are too short to reach the lock."

Gibbon said, "Let me whack it!"

Big Head declared, "It's made of iron."

Gibbon added, "Even if we reach the lock, it's no use, because Mr. Marlin locks the door from the outside.

Big Head responded, "I know from previous experience that this kind of lock can be opened from the inside."

Gibbon jumped up several times trying to reach the lock,

but with no luck. Tiny, who had been silent for a while, said, "Actually, it is easy to reach the lock."

He turned to Big Head, "You squat down and hold onto the door. You should be at the bottom because you are the strongest among us."

Then he said to Four Eyes, "Now you climb on top of Big Head and put a foot on each of his shoulders."

Big Head was impressed, "Why didn't I think of this before?"

Tiny said, "That's easy to understand! Because none of you ever dreamt that you could get out of here!"

Then he said to Gibbon, "Now, do the same as Four Eyes, and climb onto his shoulders."

After Gibbon had climbed on top of Four Eyes, Tiny said to the others, "Come and hold Big Head steady, and help him to slowly stand up."

Big Head straightened up, and so did Four Eyes. Next, Gibbon, who was on Four Eyes'shoulders, also straightened up and steadied himself by holding onto the door. No one could see anything, but all eyes were on the spot the lock was supposed to be. Gibbon tried to hold onto the door with only one hand, while reaching for the lock with his other hand.

After a while, Gibbon sighed, "I can't reach it."

The dolls were frustrated that they had failed at their attempt. There was silence.

Then, Tiny began to hum their solemn and stirring Song of Revolt:

"Wake up,
Noble dolls!

Rise up,

And fight side by side ! ..."

Still humming, Tiny climbed onto Big Head. He was small and didn't weigh very much. Big Head felt him climb effortlessly up onto his shoulders. Big Head started humming as well. All the dolls' eyes moved as Tiny sang, as if saw him climbing. They all began to sing and their voices grew louder and louder.

Tiny climbed onto Gibbon, "I hope you can stand firm on Four Eyes' shoulders and then lift me up to the lock with your hands."

Tiny finally crawled into Gibbon's hand. Gibbon lifted him up slowly. In that moment, time seemed to stop. After what seemed like a whole century had passed, in the darkness the door opened with a click.

Outside the door there was a long windy passage, and when the lock opened, the wind rushed into the room like a monster that had been trapped in a cage for a long time. The iron door clanged open in a sudden gust of strong wind. Big Head, Four Eyes, and Gibbon were knocked to the ground, while Tiny held tight with both hands to the doorknob. The light, like water being let out of a sluice gate, poured into the warehouse, which until then had been in endless darkness. The dolls couldn't adjust to the light for a moment, and they either turned their heads away or covered their eyes with their hands.

"Rush out ! "shouted Tiny, as he hung onto the doorknob.

Then, more than a hundred dolls scrambled towards the clear light and down the steps.

It was eight o'clock in the morning. Running along the corridor, the escaping dolls burst into the large doll shop where Mr. Marlin kept his selection of beautiful dolls on ten or so shelves. The lovely dolls, fast asleep on their shelves, were suddenly woken up by the sound of singing and running feet. When fully awake, they were stunned by what they saw, *Why were there so many dolls? Where did they all come from?*

The dolls on the shelves and the dolls on the floor looked at each other. The dolls on the shelves soon noticed that the dolls on the ground looked extremely hostile. They shivered unconsciously, moved backwards, and pressed themselves against the back of their shelves.

The fleeing dolls were so happy to escape from the darkness, that for a moment they didn't pay any more attention to the dolls on the shelves. The morning sun shone through six large windows onto the floor in front of the counter. There were trees outside the windows. It was windy, and the sun's rays shimmered through their swaying branches, like ripples of water. The dolls were a little intoxicated by the sunshine. Their bodies shivered with anticipation. Sunshine is so precious.

In the sunshine, the dolls looked carefully at themselves and at each other. They had lived together for a long time in the darkness, but had never really seen each other clearly. Whenever an occasional beam of light flashed through a crack in the door, they focused all their attention on the fleeting light, giving them no time to look around at their companions. Now they at last got a good look at their friends. In their eyes, all their companions were the very best dolls in the world. The girls were beautiful and the boys were handsome. Some were cute or bashful, which made the others want to kiss them on the cheeks. They hugged and praised each other. All eyes turned to Little Butterfly. She was extremely shy and lowered her eyes. Her face was a little pale because of the long absence of sunlight.

Nobody noticed as Tiny climbed onto the window sill.

Big Head said to Tiny, "You are so small, and handsome too!"

"Not just handsome! He's also brilliant!" exclaimed Four Eyes.

Turning his head and looking closely at Tiny, he continued, "And he is a little powerful ... no, not a little, he is totally powerful!"

Then their eyes returned to the dolls on the shelves. The dolls on the shelves had been quietly watching the dolls below them. Most of them were not aware that there had been a hundred of dolls locked in the basement. They didn't understand why these dolls were crazy and weird, and appeared to be resentful, angry, and aloof. They were very different from themselves, and made them nervous and uneasy.

The dolls stood motionless on the ground and looked coldly up at the dolls on the shelves. After a while, they began to feel awkward. Some climbed onto the windowsill, some climbed onto chairs, some onto the table, and then some from the table onto the counter.

On the counter, there was a potted plant. One of the dolls had a sword, and he went up to the plant and deliberately chopped it. Instantly, its leaves and two deep red flowers scattered onto the ground. Next, Big Head climbed onto the table and purposefully knocked over a water glass. The water flowed all over the table. The glass then rolled to the ground and shattered into pieces.

Big Head smiled at the dolls on the shelves, "Sorry, but that was intentional! However, it wasn't intentional towards you, because you aren't the one who locked us up in the dark!"

The dolls that had escaped from the dark warehouse suddenly had a strong desire to mercilessly destroy everything in sight! The pen holder was kicked over and the pens scattered all across the floor. The telephone wire was pulled out and the phone was thrown into the fish tank. There was a vase on the counter with colourful paper flowers in it. Two of the dolls grabbed the vase and flung it to the ground. The vase broke, and the boys picked up the flowers and gave them to the girls. Another doll found a can of paint and a paintbrush in a cupboard. He opened the can, dipped the brush deep into the paint, and scrawled all over one of the walls. Then, he picked up the can itself and splashed the rest of the paint all over another wall. Hundreds of dolls were frantically running around the room, getting madder and madder.

Little Butterfly, who had been watching from behind the curtain, grew excitement and scared.

After the dolls had made a complete mess of the room, they began to turn their attention to the dolls on the shelves, who had been watching the destruction in horror. Now they had a feeling that the dolls on the ground were going to rush onto their shelves and throw them down.

Big Head said sarcastically to them, "You all look very

comfortable up there！”

Gibbon added，“What makes you think you should stay on the shelves？”

A doll from the crowd said，“We should throw them one by one into that dark room！”

After that，the room fell silent. Some of the dolls on the shelves began to tremble. When a doll on the ground moved fiercely towards a doll on a shelf，Tiny quickly slithered down a curtain to the ground. He jumped onto a chair，then onto the table，and from there onto the counter.

Pointing to the dolls on the floor，he shouted “You are shameless！You all deserve to be locked up in that dark room again！Forever！I know what you are thinking！You want to climb the shelves and send them ...”

He turned to point to the dolls on the shelves，“You want to send them to the dark room that we were locked up in！They are innocent. They are dolls who live at the mercy of others，just like us. You should be ashamed to have such mean and rotten thoughts in your hearts. You're a bunch of cowards！We have been locked in the dark for so long that it has made us cold and heartless！”

Tiny looked down sadly and continued，“Just now，I was overjoyed to watch you madly destroy everything. But，is that what we actually want？Do we really wish to revolt and to cause destruction in this world？”

The dolls on the ground lowered their eyes in shame.

From one of the shelves，a doll cried，“The day before yesterday，I was almost thrown into the dark room too.”

Tiny looked up at the clock on the wall and sighed，“The shop opens at half past nine，and Mr. Marlin will be here very soon. If you don't watch out, he'll find you here still going crazy when he arrives and then throw you all back into the basement. Then, you'll be there until the day you die!"

Fifteen minutes later, Mr. Marlin arrived at the shop door. He was neatly dressed, and his hair was carefully combed, like a gentleman. He took the key out of his pocket, put it into the lock, but found that the door wouldn't open.

What has happened? Mr. Marlin was baffled and inserted the key into the keyhole repeatedly, for at least a dozen more times, but still failed to open the door. When he finally gave up using the key to open the door and began to think of other ways to get into the shop, he heard a song coming from inside:

"Wake up!
Noble dolls!
Rise up,
And fight side by side!..."

At first the singing was soft, and then it grew louder and louder. The steady, mournful and heroic song made Mr. Marlin uneasy and frightened. He ran to the window and peered through the glass. He was shocked by what he saw. Dozens of dolls filled the room, standing in groups, all singing at the top of their voices. And everything in the room had been completely destroyed. Mr. Marlin's eyes glanced over the faces of the dolls. He tried to think. He couldn't remember all the dolls after such a long time. However, he did recognize some of them. He recalled they were the dolls that he had abandoned in the dark warehouse. *They must have locked the door!* Mr. Marlin was very angry.

He grabbed the steel bar of a security window with one hand and yelled loudly, "What are you doing? Are you going to rebel?"

"Open the door of darkness,
We must follow the light,
Like moths! ..."

"You dolls are so ugly! You deserve to stay in there ... in the dark basement!"

"We are behind the door of death,
No escape hatches,
No time to manoeuvre,
Only to fight to the death,
On to the road to freedom ..."

"I have been selling dolls my entire life. There is no one in this city who does not know my shop! Why? Because the dolls I sell here are perfect. I recognise that I am rather harsh, even cruel, but it is all for the success of this shop!"

He commanded, "Open the door!"

"It is today,
We must bid farewell to the despair of yesterday,
Open your arms to greet tomorrow!
Tomorrow! Tomorrow!
The brilliant tomorrow! ..."

"Tomorrow! " yelled Mr. Marlin. "Your tomorrow will be in that dark room! I put you in there because I was compassionate. I could have thrown you straight into the rubbish bin. I'll give you a chance to return to the basement before I open the door. If you miss that opportunity, I'll throw you into the garbage and bury you in the sour and smelly trash. Open the door! Open the door! "

The singing didn't stop.

It was Sunday, and many people had arrived at the shop to buy dolls. When they saw the door was closed, they asked,

"Why haven't you opened the door yet? "

Mr. Marlin was embarrassed and stammered, "A group of unruly kids ... rebels ... locked the door."

The customers assumed that Mr. Marlin's children had played a joke on him and that they had locked the door. But on second thoughts, Mr. Marlin didn't have a whole "group" of kids!

"Actually, they are the ugly dolls that I rejected and left in the basement! " Mr. Marlin said.

The customers thought Mr. Marlin was crazy. The dolls? Had the dolls rebelled? Had the dolls locked the shop door?

They were confused and rushed to look through the windows. More than a hundred dolls were singing energetically. The customers couldn't believe their eyes and thought they must be dreaming. But the sky above them, the clouds, and the flying pigeons were real. The street alongside them, the buzz of passing cars, and the ringing of the bicycle bells were also real. And so, they now believed that what they had seen inside the shop was real.

They were amazed, exhilarated, and full of wonder.

Brimming with curiosity, they gathered around Mr. Marlin and inquired what had happened. As they listened, they completely forgot that it was merely dolls they heard singing. In their eyes, the dolls were an abandoned army that had been deprived of the right to life, and had finally risen up in revolt.

Mr. Marlin made a concession to the dolls, saying, "I will let you out of the basement, but only if you go back in there first. Then, I'll let you out one by one.

The dolls knew Mr. Marlin's scheme was to trick them, so they ignored him. More and more people came along to see what was going on.

Mr. Marlin, who was a proud man, felt humiliated. He pointed furiously at the dolls in the room and said, "You just wait and see!"

Pushing his way through the crowd, he walked away angrily. The dolls stopped singing.

Tiny said to others, "We must find a safe place at once! The battle begins!"

There was a stir in the crowd. One of the dolls on the shelves said, "You can climb up to the attic, which has a skylight. Then you can climb through the skylight and onto the roof."

All the dolls on the floor looked up at the attic and saw there was a ladder that led up to it. The dolls scrambled onto the ladder and started to climb up. In the rush, sometimes one of them would be knocked off the ladder and would fall back down to the ground. It was chaos!

Tiny cried out, "Stop pushing!"

But no one listened to him.

Just then, Mr. Marlin and his two strong sons arrived carrying a large plank of wood. Before the dolls had all reached the attic, Mr. Marlin and his sons started banging on the door with the wood, "Bang, bang ... "It sounded like a gun, and the building shook and trembled. As the last of dolls were starting to climb the ladder, the door of the shop fell in. It lay like a great black shadow on the floor. Tiny, who had already reached the attic, saw little Butterfly was still on the ladder and stretched out his hand to her. He was about to pull her up, but Little Butterfly slipped among the jostling crowd of dolls and fell down to the ground.

A doll on the shelves shouted, "Close the attic door quickly!" He looked very worried. Several more dolls fell off the ladder. Those who didn't fall started scrambling up as fast as they could. At that moment, Mr. Marlin and his two sons rushed into the shop. As soon as Tiny saw them, he closed the attic door, and then with the help of the other dolls, locked it.

By now, most of the dolls had climbed through the skylight and onto the roof. Those already on the roof helped the others by pulling them up as quickly as they could. Once up there, they saw that their roof was connected to many others, and therefore they would be able to escape in all directions.

However, the dolls on the roof didn't want to leave without those who had not yet escaped. They thought they had probably been taken back to the dark basement.

From the rooftop, the dolls could see for miles and miles. They saw the pale white clouds in the sky above, and the streets below. It was noon, and the bright midday sun shone down on the earth. For a moment they forgot that they were still in danger, and that some of their companions were still in darkness. They were so happy and excited about their freedom that they ran around dancing with glee.

Tiny sat alone on the ridge of the house, with his hands around his knees. He was thinking of what had just happened a moment ago, when Little Butterfly had fallen off the ladder. And how, as she fell, her hands had reached out to him and her eyes had looked helplessly up at him.

With the plank of wood, Mr. Marlin and his sons now started to bang heavily on the attic door. But because it was so high up, it was difficult for them to break through.

Even though the door was not opening, each vibration really scared the dolls.

Big Head said, "Let's run!"

Tiny stood up and announced, "We can't go! We still have dozens of friends who are not free! If we leave, they might never get another chance at freedom. Don't forget that we all spent a lot of time in the darkness together. We can't leave any of them behind!" He looked down at the streets below and saw people approaching from all directions.

"Don't be afraid. Look! More and more people are coming. Let us sing our song so that they can hear the truth about our situation."

Four Eyes sang first:

> "Wake up,
> Noble dolls!
> Rise up,
> And fight side by side!..."

29

In a while, the others joined in the chorus.

In no time at all, the news of the revolt of the dolls had spread throughout the city streets. An endless stream of people came to see what was going on. Mr. Marlin and his two sons were shocked to see so many people outside their windows. After thinking for a few moments, they put down the wooden plank.

"Dad, maybe you are wrong!" the eldest child said.

"I think so," the younger son agreed.

Mr. Marlin sank onto a chair.

The police arrived! Four or five police cars with their lights flashing were parked on the nearby street. Mr. Marlin walked out of the shop with his head down. All eyes turned to him in bewilderment and condemnation.

Meanwhile, the dolls walked to the lower part of the roof so that everyone could see them.

Everyone in the crowd below-men, women, the young, and the old-admired the dolls.

"Beautiful!"

"So lovely!"

"I'd be so lucky if I had such a doll!"

A little boy pointed to Gibbon and said to his father, "Daddy, I like him!"

Another little boy pointed to a doll with a sword and said to his mother, "Mummy, let's take him home."

A girl in her mother's arms who just learned to talk, pointed to a blond-haired doll, saying, "Mummy, I want her!"

Now, the mayor of the city arrived.

He asked, "Who is Mr. Marlin?"

Mr. Marlin came up and answered, "It's me!"

"You are Mr. Marlin?" The mayor looked at him, nodded sarcastically, and then whispered, "I am ashamed that my city has a citizen such as you!"

"Mr. Mayor, are you saying that my actions over all these years have been a mistake?"

"Not a mistake, but a crime!" The mayor looked up at the roof, saying, "I feel very sorry for those poor dolls up there."

The police brought out a large sheet of canvas. Then, many of the citizens seized the edges of the canvas and helped the police unfold it into a large square.

Everyone shouted to the dolls, "Jump! Just jump! Don't be afraid! No one will hurt you now."

The dolls continued singing.

The mayor took a megaphone from a policeman, and said loudly to the dolls on the roof, "All men are created equal, and so are you! Jump! I promise that all the people of this city will protect you. Each one of them will be happy to take you home with them! One loving family after another awaits you!"

Still the dolls remained on the roof.

Mr. Marlin walked to the mayor with his head down, and said, "Mr. Mayor, I know why they don't want to jump."

He went back to the shop with his two sons, where they took all the dolls out of the dark basement, brought them outside, and laid them gently on the canvas. The dolls on the roof examined the scene carefully, and after making sure that all the dolls were free, they celebrated.

The dolls on the canvas jumped up and cheered at the dolls on the roof.

Little Butterfly skipped and cried with relief.

At last, one of the dolls jumped down from the roof onto the canvas. Then, one by one, the others followed. Immediately, people gathered around and scrambled to pick up the dolls for themselves. Before long the canvas bed was empty.

The crowd began to leave.

An hour later, everyone was gone.

Mr. Marlin, with his head in his hands, crouched down by the wall and sobbed.

An old woman with a walking stick approached from nearby. She was dressed in rags, and the wrinkles on her face formed deep folds. Her hair was grey and white, and when the wind blew, it sparked in the sun. She had watery eyes that she wiped with the edge of her sleeve. A basket was slung over her arm.

On noticing someone standing in front of him, Mr. Marlin looked up.

The old woman asked in an old husky voice, "May I have the doll?"

Mr. Marlin looked around. There were none left. He said, "They have all been taken."

The old woman pointed to the nearby grass, "There is one left."

Tiny was standing there.

A little boy had taken him, but when he had seen another larger doll, he dropped Tiny onto the grass. He was so small that the grass covered him.

Mr. Marlin saw Tiny and said to the old women, "You can ask him if he wants to go with you."

The old woman bent down and asked Tiny, "I'm just an old beggar who has nothing. But I like you. Would you like to come with me?"

Tiny walked slowly through the grass until he was standing at the feet of the old woman.

The old woman stretched out her arms, picked him up, and hugged him. Then they walked slowly away together along Blue Tile Street. It was four o'clock in the afternoon and the sun's rays cast a shimmer of light down the street ...

Modified on September 4, 2013

The Ships on the Sea

The wind blows the white clouds that scatter across the sky, causing them to constantly change shape. Down below, the waves in the deep blue sea roll gently, like an endless scroll of thick, soft blue silk. The sun shines radiantly down from above, its golden rays bouncing across the water.

Haizai lowered his head and walked along the beach. The sea breeze blew against his face, hair and clothes. Behind him, he left a row of twisted footprints in the damp sand. Too tired to walk any further, he sat down on the beach, and felt the rising sea water ebb and flow onto his outstretched legs.

Looking far into the distance, he saw a very tall white sail that looked like the giant wings of a large bird pointing straight upward to the clouds. It was a spectacular sight. Haizai had grown up by the seaside, and he liked ships. But he only liked the ships that sailed on the sea. Once, he had gone with his mother to visit his uncle, and his little cousin had announced very proudly that there was a ship on the small river in front of their house. Haizai went to look at it and thought, *Hey! This is a so-called ship! It's no more than a big bathtub!*

"The ships on our sea are enormous!" he said contemptuously, pointing at the boat on the river. "Your boat is like an egg that has been laid by a big ship!"

A ship is very grand, tall, and long. When its massive sail

is up, it cuts rapidly through the waves and flies across the sea at high speed. It can sail far beyond the horizon and reach very distant lands.

"Dad, why are the ships on the sea so big, and why is the boat on the river so small? "At that time, he was only four years old, just a little boy.

Dad smiled.

Mother answered him, "The sea is wide, vast! It is enormous, has great strength, and can accommodate and carry huge ships. The river is narrow and small. It cannot accommodate the large ships that sail on the sea."

He nodded repeatedly, and seemed to understand.

Now, he is twelve years old, and wonders what it is today that he doesn't seem to understand.

One

But, don't look down on this little guy ... for he had once captured forty-nine young hearts!

When he was in the first year of primary school, Haizai was a respected hero among the children. On the first day of school, he stole a football from the office, took it outside, and started to play with his classmates. The PE teacher found out and stormed outside to the playground. At that very second, as the football flew straight at him, he stopped it with one foot. He kicked the ball into the air with one foot and skilfully reached out his hand and caught it, before looking seriously at the children. The children watched him with admiration, but not one of them dared to ask him to give the ball back to them.

No one, that is, except Haizai! He did dare! He rushed

up to the PE teacher, "We want to play football!"

The PE teacher pushed him gently away from him.

He was stunned and ran to the PE teacher again, "We want to play football!"

The PE teacher again pushed him away, "First year kids aren't allowed to play football!"

He stood and watched the teacher take the football away. After a few minutes, Haizai was seen standing in front of the school on the tall stone rock that overlooked the sea. The waves crashed against the cliff, and the rapids under the reef swirled, making a howling sound, like a hungry beast. The children crowded beneath the high stone rock and looked up nervously. The teachers joined them, "You ...!"

Haizai said stubbornly, "We first-years want to play football!" He walked step by step towards the edge of the rock, scaring everyone. The onlookers, wide-eyed and open-mouthed, stared nervously.

"No ... Stop!" shouted Mr. Guo, the elderly tutor. His hands shook and his face turned pale with fear.

"If you don't give us a football to play with, I will jump into the sea!" Haizai continued to move towards the edge of the rock. Another step forward, and he would fall into the raging current.

"Okay, okay!" the PE teacher conceded. And he quickly threw the football at the group of first-years.

What a boy! He had conquered his forty-nine classmates' young hearts with his boldness, courage and zeal. From first grade through fifth grade, all the students chose him as their leader!

But now, as the children grew older, they didn't like

Haizai as much as they had before. He had become too powerful, looked down on them, and was often arrogant. They grumbled and began to plan a secret revolt.

When the class election began, they voted for Shanshan, a shy and quiet girl who blushed before she even spoke her first word in public, to be their class prefect. As Mr. Guo announced the voting results, the children exhaled sighs of relief. Applause erupted in the classroom and a group of boys shouted, "Oh, oh, oh, " with satisfaction.

Haizai slammed his hands angrily onto the podium. Holding his head high, he bit his trembling lips.

The children looked at him in silence.

They realised the unbearable pain their actions had brought to their former prefect. Embarrassed, they turned their eyes away from him.

Some children felt sorry for him. In their hearts, they remembered what a good person Haizai had once been; how he had always stood up for the younger and weaker students, protecting them from older bullies. He would rush up, wave his fists, and make them stop. They also remembered some fun adventures he led them on, like the time on a dark night when he had led them onto a fishing boat and they had hid among the fishing nets. The boat had set sail along the coast by the time the adults found out! There was nothing to be done! There was no other choice but to let them play out at sea for two days until the boat went ashore! *Yes*, they thought, *he has done many good things for us.*

Other children were complacent, some were indifferent, and one was angry, shouting, "What are you doing? You're being so pitiful just because you're no longer a prefect!"

Haizai felt his eyes fill with tears. He, the former prefect Haizai, never wanted to let the children see him cry. What a disgrace that would be! He picked up his bag, put his hands on his hips, dashed out of the classroom, and ran from the school.

His tutor Mr. Guo shook his head repeatedly and thought, What a baby!

Two

Haizai refused to enter the school gates again. Would he take orders from the "little girl", allow students to stick their tongues out at him and make faces behind his back?

No way!

In the past, early each morning, more than a dozen children would wait at his door and follow him to school. Once, when he injured his leg, the children had turned over a desk for him to sit on, hoisted it up with bamboo poles, and carried him to school. He had had an entourage! But now, no one, except for Heitou, came near him.

Heitou gave many a headache to the headmaster and teachers. He was a mischievous prankster and a troublemaker. But he was absolutely loyal and obedient to Haizai, always doing as he asked. Whenever Haizai gave the word, Heitou obeyed without hesitation, as if it were a matter of life or death. Haizai was especially protective of him. When he got into trouble, Haizai would lie for him, or simply become his scapegoat. When Haizai had been the prefect, Heitou had got away with anything. He had been as free as a fish in the sea. Now that Haizai had been forced "to step down," he was disappointed and sad. Others had forgotten Haizi, but although he too tried to forget Haizai, he couldn't. Unfortunately, nowadays Haizai was always angry and ignored him. There was nothing Heitou could do but droop his head and walk away.

With no company, Haizai felt despondent and went to wander around the village.

In the village, the adults were very busy, either preparing to go out to sea or making and mending fishing nets. The leaves of the trees swayed and swished in the sea breeze. A few dogs meandered slowly through the village.

The first day passed, then the second, and on the third day Haizai grew a little impatient. He found a wooden stick and pretended to be a soldier, waving it around like a sword and commanding his army of reeds. After a while, he grew bored and threw the wooden stick onto the beach. Then, he leaned against a tall tree, sank down, and sat listlessly at its base.

The sea water came up from over the horizon: layer by layer of water, creating a swell of waves. The water lapped against the shore, rushed up, and retreated endlessly, with a "swish, swish, swish!"

Monotonous, extremely monotonous!

When had Haizai ever been all alone? He was the "leader" with a band of followers! But now, he was a loner!

As he sat beneath the tree, a group of butt naked children rushed onto the beach shouting, "Go, kill!"

Haizai looked at the ringleader of the group. He was a swaggering flat-nosed boy, with hatred in his heart. The other children skipped excitedly around him.

Haizai watched them for a while, and then beckoned to them, "Hey, come here, come over here!"

The children looked over, ignored him, and continued playing their games. Haizai lay down on the beach. The butt naked "army", under the command of the flat-nosed boy, played around him. He got up, rushed at the children, took a deep breath and asked, "Can I be in charge?"

The children looked at him and one by one shook their heads, "No! No!" They grabbed small wooden sticks and bamboo poles, and ran off into the distance.

Haizai ran after them and grabbed hold of the flat-nosed boy. His friends were scared and stopped running.

"Will you let me take command?" he urged threateningly, shaking his fists.

"No!" retorted the flat-nosed boy.

In unison, the other children shouted, "No!"

There was nothing Hazai could do, and so he let go of the flat-nosed boy. Then, putting his hand into his trouser pocket, he felt something under his finger tips and quickly pulled it out. When he saw what he had in his hand he shouted joyfully, "I have a lot of jellybeans!"

The children stopped running, turning their heads to look first at Haizai and then at each other. One little guy gulped hungrily and moved a few steps forward. The others began to push forward too. They stood on tiptoe, staring at the colourful jellybeans in his hand.

Haizai walked forward, and the children followed closely behind.

Turning he head, he ordered, "Line up!"

The children obeyed and formed a queue in front of him.

He put two jellybeans into each of their small dirty hands. After handing out the jellybeans, he picked up the flat-nosed boy's wooden stick from the sand and commanded, "Follow me!"

Happily chewing their jellybeans, the children followed their new "commander" along the beach.

He was happy!

Although Haizai was exhausted, on that day his heart was full of joy.

Over the next three or four days, he stole eggs from his chicken coop and exchanged them for jellybeans in the small village shop. But, after a few days, Haizai got tired of playing with the children. They cried, lay on the ground like spoilt babies, and continually stretched out their small hands for more jellybeans. He realised that without jellybeans to bribe them with, they wouldn't follow his orders and treat him as their leader.

One day, the children left the beach without a trace, leaving Haizai all alone there again. There was no wind, and the sea was calm and quiet. He picked up some tiles and skimmed them across the surface of the water. He felt listless and tired and fell down on the sand. A lone gray seagull hovered above his head.

The next day, he carried his school bag and small bench and went back to school.

Three

On his return to school, Haizai was very arrogant. He walked around with a sarcastic look on his face, and behaved as if he were always ready to embarrass and mock others.

In PE class, he deliberately kicked the ball outside the fence. He refused to go and fetch it, and instead, climbed up onto the goal post and sat proudly on top of it. When others worked, he lay on his desk and swung his legs. No one dared to criticize him.

As for Shanshan, he really looked down on to her.

When she distributed the homework books and accidentally dropped some of them on the ground, Haizai said contemptuously, "Can't you even hand out books properly? "

On another occasion, Shanshan couldn't read Heitou's name on the front of his book because his handwriting was so untidy.

Haizai jeered, "Can't you read? "

Haizai didn't understand why he behaved this way, and teased the new prefect over and over again, making her feel very awkward. But Shanshan was no pushover. She remained calm, and time after time ignored him. However, one day she had at last had enough! When Haizai refused to write a contribution for the classroom blackboard journal, she got very angry and yelled, "If you don't complete it before the school is over, I'll make a note tonight so that you will be publicly criticised tomorrow morning during tutorial time! "

"I don't want to write! " Haizai's nose was out of joint and he was angry.

As soon as the class was over, the students saw Heitou put two sheets of folded paper onto the board. They rushed over, and found it was Haizai's work. A few children climbed onto the table and looked down, laughing at Haizai, who was nonchalantly lying back in his chair.

"Do you think I am afraid of her?" He continued, "I can write when I want to!"

The children laughed louder.

One morning, a school assembly was held on the playground. The classes were led outside by their prefects. However, the fifth grade was nowhere in sight! It was discovered that someone had locked the door and they couldn't get out of their classroom!

The voice of the PE teacher boomed angrily over the loudspeaker system, "Where is the fifth grade? All the other classes are here!"

Shanshan's face turned red with embarrassment. In the end, the fifth-graders had to climb out of the window. They sped hurriedly to the playground, where all the other students had been standing for the past fifteen minutes.

The PE teacher looked furious.

"Stand up! Stand up straight!" Shanshan's forehead was dripping with sweat as she ran from the front to the back of the line, trying to get her students to line up properly.

Heitou meandered over slowly and was still about ten meters away from his classmates. Haizai stood at a distance, his arms crossed and his head held high. The troublemakers ... those boys who disapproved of having a girl in charge of them ... deliberately pushed and shoved other students, yelling noisily, and generally making a big fuss.

"Shanshan, what on earth is happening?" asked the PE teacher angrily. "Look at your team, untidy, and curving like a snake!"

The children in the other classes laughed.

Heitou's laughter was louder than anyone else's.

Shanshan, who was very shy, lowered her head. She bit her lip and tears welled up in her eyes.

As soon as the assembly was over, she ran into the office and said to Mr. Guo, "I don't want to be a prefect anymore!"

Mr. Guo comforted her and said encouragingly, "Come now, everyone chose you."

Shanshan left his office and Mr. Guo stormed furiously along to the classroom. Heitou had a feeling there would be trouble. The students sat quiet and still, trying to give the impression that nothing troublesome had happened.

"Who locked the door? "Mr. Guo's eyes peered over the top of his glasses.

The children all looked at Heitou. Mr. Guo's eyes scanned the room until they landed on Heitou. Heitou hadn't realised before that their normally calm teacher could be so strict and harsh. He began to panic and beads of sweat formed on his forehead.

Haizai suddenly stood up and declared, "I locked the door!"

Mr. Guo stared at him, his face turning white with anger, his chin trembling, and commanded, "Go to the office, at once!"

Haizai sauntered out of the classroom.

Four

Only the sea knew: the children and Haizai were going to launch a small "coup"!

That night, the air was moist and had a salty smell. The sky was filled with stars. In the distance and out at sea the lights of fishing boats flickered. There was no wind and the water was calm.

Several children sat restlessly on the beach under a big tree.

As they sat there, they began to plot how they could bring even more embarrassment to Shanshan.

At 10 o'clock the following morning, senior students from several fishing village schools were to compete against each other in a boat race that would start at the beach and end at Wolf Island. The first team to arrive at Wolf Island would be declared the winner.

Haizai sat with his knees tucked under him and looking silently out to sea. He knew what Heitou wanted to do. Of course he would not stop him. He had mixed emotions, and was both excited and apprehensive at the same time.

Heitou announced his plan. "Tomorrow, when the race begins, we'll take up our oars and pretend to row as hard and as fast as possible. But really, we'll make sure the boat only moves very slowly, just like a sea turtle! "

"Shanshan won't let us row, "one child said doubtfully.

Heitou didn't say anything.

"We shouldn't do this! "another child said.

"Mr. Guo will punish us. You've seen how angry he can get! He's really strict! "

They couldn't think of anything else, and they didn't say anything for a while.

Haizai's heart was thumping. He had an idea, but for some reason, he didn't want to tell the others.

The children noticed and asked him, "Do you have an idea? "

He bit his lip.

45

"Tell us!" Heitou urged.

"What are you afraid of?" demanded someone.

This made Haizai mad. "I am not afraid!" He pointed to the boat moored in the bay. "Are we using that boat tomorrow? We can ..."

Without waiting for him to finish his words, Heitou interrupted, "Yes, we will loosen the oar locks!" (Oar locks are braces fixed to the side of a boat that hold the oars in place and prevent them from falling into the water. They enable rowers to move through the water using small and smooth rowing movements.)

The children looked around cautiously. While others were sleeping, the mysterious sea seemed to be quietly listening to them.

The little conspirators went home. The sea wind blew. Behind them they heard the sound of the restless waves. Above them, the stars were beginning to fade in the night sky.

Haizai tossed and turned in his bed, trying his best to convince himself that his idea of loosening the oar locks was the right thing to do.

The competition began, and the three boats sailed out to sea towards Wolf Island. The island was shaped like a wolf, pouncing in readiness to attack. After a while, Shanshan's boat fell behind the others. The oar locks had come loose and their oars waved about and were impossible to control. They just slammed up and down on the water.

Shanshan cried in despair.

Oh, the captain was crying!

When the other schools' boats arrived at Wolf Island,

Shanshan's boat was only halfway there. They came in last.

The teacher asked Shanshan, "What were you doing？"

The children said, "Shanshan shouldn't have been in charge. If Haizai had been the captain we would have been guaranteed to come in first！"

Then Heitou shouted out, "We want Haizi to be our prefect！"

Haizai held his head high ... he felt so proud.

"Haizai！Haizai！" Someone was calling to him from outside his window. He woke up from his dream.

Five

Why were the ships on the sea so big？

Haizai opened the window and saw it was Shanshan.

Haizai blushed, took a deep breath, and without looking at her, asked, "What's the matter？"

Shanshan approached the windowsill. She smiled quietly and graciously, and her eyes were full of sincerity, "Today's the competition, and you will be the captain."

"What about you？" Haizai asked.

"I will cheer you on," Shanshan said shyly.

Haizai lowered his eyes. He didn't know why, but he felt embarrassed.

Shanshan also lowered her eyes, and wondered if Haizai were going to refuse her suggestion.

"I don't want to be the captain！" Haizai said stubbornly.

Shanshan looked up. There was disappointment and sadness in her eyes, "Why？"

Haizai didn't know how to answer her, and looked back down.

They both fell silent.

When Haizai at last looked up at Shanshan, he saw a pure light in her dark eyes that he had never seen before. Her eyes told him that she didn't hate him at all. She seemed to have forgiven him for everything. He never wanted to see that look in her eyes again. He closed the window. When he looked up, Shanshan had already walked away. He threw open the window and stared out blankly.

He ran out of the house to the beach. Slowing down to a walk, he bit his lip, kicked some shells, and hit his forehead with his fist. A while later, tired out, he flung himself down onto the sand.

He didn't know how much time had passed, when Heitou came running frantically towards him.

Panting, and out of breath, he said, "Where have you been? We've been looking everywhere for you! Be quick … go … if we are late, we can't enter the race!"

Heitou pushed Haizai, "They are waiting for you."

Haizai remained on the sand, like a piece of wet driftwood.

Heitou scoffed, "You coward!"

Haizai leapt up and threw a punch at Heitou's chest.

Heitou was stunned and looked very confused.

Haizai glared at Heitou. Heitou glared back at him, then turned and ran away.

Haizai sat back down on the sand.

The sea shimmered and sparkled in the sunlight. Seagulls flew freely across the sky. A ship approached, its head held high on the open sea, its white sail like a curtain before his eyes. Far away on the horizon, where the sea and sky merge into one, he saw many more ships.

Haizai stared into the distance: Why are the ships on the sea so big?

Written in August, 1980
Revised on September 28, 2013

Rosewood–coloured Skin

Chenchen announced to his classmates, "My dad is taking me to the beach as soon as summer holiday starts！"

He stood on top of a concrete table tennis table that had a missing corner. His excessive excitement made him stammer and stutter, so that some of his words weren't clear. When he finished speaking, he gulped nervously and jumped off the table tennis table like a flustered rooster.

The children in this school worshipped the sea. Every summer, some of them went to the seaside for their holidays. Almost two-thirds of the children in Chenchen's class had been to the seaside, although some of them had to spend a lot of time relentlessly begging their parents to take them there.

The schoolchildren admired the rosewood-coloured skin that was acquired after spending time at the beach. The tanned skin looked as if it were coated with a layer of glaze and gave off a lovely glow. The effect of seawater, the sunshine, and the sea breeze made the skin look soft and smooth, almost like polished copper. All the children thought that rosewood-coloured skin was extremely beautiful.

At the end of every summer holiday, when those children who came back from the beach with tanned and shining skin began to talk about their experiences, Chenchen would silently walk away. He couldn't stand to see their gorgeous skins, their arrogant expressions, and their cock-a-hoop way of speaking. What drove him crazy was that all the girls liked this kind of skin, including his deskmate Qinqin, who had been to the seaside last year. As the weather grew colder, she still wore short sleeves and skirts. Chenchen thought she was intentionally exposing and showing off her fading rosewood-coloured skin. He shrugged indignantly and said to himself, *That tanning does not make people look pretty at all*!

Despite this, Chenchen had begged his father to take him to the beach. But his father was only interested in fishing, and was indifferent to his son's tears, his pleading voice, and the look of longing in his eyes. And so, Chenchen never mentioned it again.

Then, quite unexpectedly one day, his father announced, "I have fifteen days off work, and I will take you to the seaside!"

Chenchen almost cried with excitement as he ran to school.

When his summer holiday began, Chenchen waited in anticipation for the day of their departure. However, as the days went by, it seemed that his father had forgotten his promise. He didn't want to annoy him in case he took back his promise, so he kept quiet.

After waiting a few more days, he saw his father collecting his fishing gear and asked, "Daddy, when do we leave?"

"To go where?"

"To the beach!"

"Oh, we won't be going there after all. Uncle Wu has asked me to go fishing in the reservoir with him. There is plenty of fish there, and I'll be staying for ten days."

Chenchen's lips quivered like two trembling leaves, and

through a curtain of tears, his piercing look of dismay sent a shiver down his dad's spine.

Chenchen turned and fled from the room. He went outside and walked from shop to shop, from street to street, sometimes standing at the roadside vacantly watching the passing cars, and sometimes sitting on the steps of a hotel looking up at the pigeons flying by. Later, as he walked by an iron fence, he absent-mindedly ran his hands meaninglessly along each bar. By the time he went home, it was very dark.

The next day, he went to a river outside the city. He took off all his clothes and threw himself into the water. He swam for a while, then lay on the bank in the sun and daubed himself with mud. It was so hot that the sweat on his forehead glistened. Whenever he felt thirsty, he drank some water and then lay back down in the sun.

Nearby, a boy about seven or eight years old was catching small fish with a glass bottle. After he saw Chenchen on the bank, he also lay down, crossing his arms comfortably over his stomach.

Chenchen turned and smiled at the little boy.

The boy smiled back.

They made friends with each other. Every day, Chenchen went to swim in the river and to bask in the sunshine. The little boy went too.

The days went by, and Chenchen's skin blistered, peeled off, and turned red and dark. He thought the colour of his skin was not dark enough, so he persevered in going to sunbathe by the river until the very last day of his holiday. He looked at his skin and smiled with satisfaction thinking, *It is not only the seaside that can give people beautiful rosewood-*

coloured skin, *but a simple riverbank can as well*!

Wearing only shorts, he was very happy as he walked whistling merrily down the street. His friend, the little boy, also wearing only shorts, strode in step alongside him.

Chenchen managed to scrape together enough money to buy four shells from an old woman's stall.

It was time to return to school. Chenchen washed his skin with clean water and felt very nervous as he arrived at the school gate. He tightened his belt, held his head high, and entered. The sun shone down on him and his skin glistened like silk. The other children couldn't take their eyes off him.

He felt confident and jumped onto the table tennis table again and called out to the children around him, "I went to the beach, just look at my skin!"

He turned his body around like a model, and told them all about the seaside (from information he had read in books and heard in songs); the gulls, the beach, the look and sound of the waves, the white sails, and so on. As he spoke, it seemed as if he had actually seen the sea. His eyes sparkled and danced with delight. At the end of his speech, he wept with emotion, and said, "The sea, I saw the sea …"

He took the four shells out of his pocket and looked at the fascinated children saying, "I picked them up at the beach."

When Qinqin came up to him, he held up the shells, one by one. They glittered in the sun and gave off a jewel-like luster. The children looked up at the shells as if they were stars in the sky. He gave the brightest one to Qinqin.

Qinqin happily held the shell in her hand.

Chenchen enthusiastically threw the other three shells into

the crowd, yelling,

"Catch!"

The children scrambled all at once to try to get one.

Chenchen suddenly saw that his new little friend was watching him carefully. He avoided the boy's scornful look and began to run away.

Then, the little boy called out to the crowd, "He lied! He didn't go to the seaside, but got his tan lying by the river!"

The children stopped fighting and stared at Chenchen.

The little boy felt Chenchen, because of his lies, had betrayed their friendship.

"He bought his shells from a market stall!" he continued.

There was silence.

Qinqin looked at Chenchen and threw the shell at his feet. And, one after another, the other three shells were also flung back at him.

The children left, and Chenchen was alone. He stood on the table tennis table for a long time before climbing down and leaving the school. Tears were stinging in his eyes.

When he got home and saw his father's fishing gear, he wanted to throw it out of the window, bit by bit.

Written in May, 1985
Modified on September 30, 2013

The Disgusting Dwarf

The Family on the West Side

Pika really wanted to go to the house on the west side of Yau Ma Tei Primary School.

When Pika was young, he spent many days in that house, which used to be a kindergarten. His aunt was a kindergarten teacher, and so as both a kindergarten student and his aunt's nephew, he received double amount of care and attention as the other students did! Student Pika sang, played, and studied with the other children. Nephew Pika had the freedom to do whatever he wanted! Sometimes, he ran off to his grandmother's house to ask for food, and then went to play with the children in the yard of Yau Ma Tei Primary School, before returning to his kindergarten class to annoy his aunt!

Just before Pika set off to the house on the west side, Grandma warned, "Pika, don't go there!"

In the eyes of the people of Yau Ma Tei, the family of three who now occupied the house were monsters.

The man of the house was named Li Damao. For six months of the year he worked in Yau Ma Tei, and for the other six months he worked elsewhere.

Every year around the Qingming Festival, Li Damao would get stricken with a kind of madness. He would be his normal self on one day, and then overnight, for no apparent reason, when he woke up he would be totally insane!

When he met people, he would stare at them with eyes open wide, showing no signs of recognition. He would wander in the fields aimlessly like a lost soul. Sometimes he would gaze up at the sky for ages, and when he saw a bird flying above he would point up at it and giggle stupidly, like a little child. Li Damao would also throw his few possessions into the river, leaving his house completely empty. His long-suffering wife would follow him and rescue what she could from the river, but there were always some things that drifted away. She was often seen dragging a quilt or a pot from the water with a stick. Every so often, Li Damao would lie down motionless on the road, looking like a dead person. At times he would starve himself and wouldn't eat or drink for quite some time, growing so weak that he could hardly walk. A few days before he recovered from his madness, Li Damao often exhibited extremely violent behavior. He would bash his own head hard against a tall tree until its leaves fell off onto the ground. Next, he would start attacking others. However, he didn't attack just anyone, but only his wife and foolish son. He would beat them so badly that, bloodied and screaming, they would scamper away like frightened rats.

Then all of a sudden, one morning he would be his old self again!

He would wash his clothes and dress neatly, and give a friendly greeting to everyone he met. He would clean his house: sweep the floor, wipe the table, and wash the bed quilt.

He liked to visit my Grandpa's house, and would ask my Grandma, "Do you have any jobs for me?"

Grandpa's family would gave him a lot of tough and dirty

jobs, such as transporting away the waste from the toilet and re-paving the road in front of the house. Li Damao would work tirelessly, never slacking, and only stopping when my Grandma took him a bowl of water. He would always drink the water in one quick gulp because he didn't want to stop for long and delay the work. He would drink so quickly that water dribbled from the corners of his mouth and down his neck. When Grandma paid him, he would always say that it was too much.

But Grandma would insist, and he'd say gratefully, "Thank you Grandma! Thank you!"

He would apologise again and again to the neighbours and to the villagers for all the stupid things his foolish son had done.

He would spend all the money he earned on his wife and son, buying them new clothes and meat. During those times, his foolish son was very obedient and rarely behaved badly.

At that time, this family was the happiest in all of Yau Ma Tei.

When summer arrived, Li Damao would pack his things. Before leaving, he would always make sure he said goodbye to Pika's grandparents. Then, he wouldn't be back again until the end of the year.

It seemed like forever before he came home. On his return, his large woven bag was always bulging with goodies. There were new clothes for his wife and son to wear during New Year, as well as a variety of food, including some that he had picked himself while working outside.

Before he got home, his wife and foolish son would have

finished all the food that he had left for them.

During the New Year, Li Damao's family always had fish and meat to eat, wine to drink, and firecrackers to light.

Spring was on its way and the Qingming Festival was about to begin.

Suddenly one morning, Li Damao went crazy again ...

Then he recovered, and when summer arrived he went off to work again.

Li Damao had brought his wife back with him from a place where he had worked in the north. It was an evening at the end of that particular year when she arrived in Yau Ma Tei. At the time, it was snowing and everything was white. This woman, short and fat, wore a thick red jacket and looked to the people of Yau Ma Tei like a big red ball rolling slowly around on the snow.

Li Damao told the townspeople her name more than once. It was a very elegant name that didn't suit her at all! So, nobody could ever remember her name, and knowing she was rather a silly woman, called her "Mrs. Silly," both to her face and behind her back. Although she knew it was an insulting name, she nevertheless always responded to it.

At first, the people of Yau Ma Tei didn't grasp that she was a little mad, but simply thought she was different, possibly because she came from the north. Nobody understood a word she said and so just shook their heads when she spoke. Likewise, she didn't understand the language of the Yau Ma Tei locals. They looked upon each other as strangers. Many years later, the community still didn't think she belonged.

She was extremely lazy and never did any work. The house was so dirty and untidy that visitors wondered where Li

Damao could even sit down when he came home from work.

Day after day she did nothing but stand for hours on end by the fence, gazing into the distance as if she were waiting for someone to appear.

When other families held funerals, celebrations, or banquets, she was always there. She never spoke, but stood silently in the middle of the guests, looking silly. As others ate and drank, it made them feel awkward and uncomfortable.

Someone would say, "Go home!"

However, she would refuse to leave until everyone else had gone home.

When Li Damao went crazy, he would beat her up very badly. She would run and hide in other people's hayricks or pig pens, and often scare them unintentionally when they found her.

Before Li Daoma went away to work, he would always leave enough food for his wife and stupid son. If they had been normal people, they would have eaten the food gradually so that it lasted until his return. But his wife only knew how to live in the present and couldn't look to the future. So Mrs. Silly and her stupid son would do nothing but eat, eat, and eat until the grain store was exhausted, even though it was a very long time before Li Damao would be home. When there was nothing left of the grain for them to eat, they would eat the chicken that was to be saved for the Chinese New Year, as well as all the wild vegetables and fallen fruits they could find. When the son got extremely hungry, he would get very angry and beat his mother. Occasionally, some kind villagers would give them some food. However, whenever Li Damao returned home, his wife and son would be almost too thin and weak to stand.

The woman had given birth to their son in the autumn of her second year in Yau Ma Tei.

In the beginning, nobody thought anything was wrong with the child, but by the time he was three years old, the townspeople came to the conclusion that he was a simpleton.

The boy had originally been given a good name, Li Dapeng, which meant anyone with that name would have a bright future and long life. But soon, no one called him that as it just didn't seem to match his character. Up to the age of ten, everyone called him "fool." After he was ten, they changed his name to "the disgusting dwarf" and had called him that ever since. Now he was fourteen years old.

At first, they called him "dwarf" because he was a lot shorter than a normal child of his age. Even though he was fourteen, he was shorter than Pika. They also thought that "dwarf" was a more interesting name than "fool." When they first called him "fool," they had still had a little sympathy and compassion in their hearts for him, thinking to themselves that there were many names that could be much worse than "fool." To the people of Yau Ma Tei however, the change of name to "dwarf" now expressed their feelings of discomfort, disgust, and hatred towards him.

The disgusting dwarf wandered around Yau Ma Tei at all times of the day and night, appearing and disappearing in and out of the shadows like a ghost. He still couldn't count the number of fingers on his hands, but had the ability to behave more badly and destructively than all of the children of Yau

Ma Tei put together. Wherever he went, he created turmoil and chaos.

Sometimes, he sneaked into the orchard, picked the green apples from more than ten apple trees, and scattered them all over the ground. The apples, still tiny and growing, would no longer be available to harvest in the autumn.

In the moonlight, the dwarf went to the watermelon field carrying a thin wooden stick. He walked around piercing the watermelons one by one, delighting in the squelching and squishing sounds each one made. Nobody noticed anything was wrong until the harvest season came along and they saw that every single one of them was rotten.

He climbed up onto house roofs and destroyed chimneys, so that when people started cooking the smoke couldn't escape and their houses filled with smoke. Choking and coughing, they had to escape outside.

Whenever people saw him coming, they would observe him with caution and warn everyone, "The disgusting dwarf is coming!"

The adults would use him to scare their disobedient children, "The disgusting dwarf is coming!" This made them instantly stop their bad behaviour.

He looked like a phantom as he strolled about. He would stand still, slowly turn his head, and look around with eyes as white as porcelain.

Rarely did anyone hear him talk. He was like a dumb mute. However, there was someone who knew that he was perfectly capable of speaking. Grandpa had once heard him talking to a lizard, speaking many words fluently and full of emotion.

Grandpa told the teachers at Yau Ma Tei Primary School,

"Not too many children in the school can speak as well as the dwarf can."

Still, he kept his mouth shut and never spoke. This made Li Damao very angry.

He pulled off the belt from around his waist and whipped the dwarf, yelling, "Speak! Open your mouth and speak, otherwise I will kill you!" The dwarf stood in the corner facing the wall and still did not speak.

Incredibly, the dwarf never behaved badly when he was at Yau Ma Tei Primary School. Not only did he not do bad things, but if he saw anyone damaging the school property, he would attack them relentlessly, throwing bricks at them and hitting them with a stick. Once, a down-and-out picked a flower from the school garden. The dwarf chased him for a long way before catching up with him. Then, he took back the flower and flung the man's bag on the ground with such force that all its contents spilled out onto the ground.

Although the dwarf was short, he was extremely strong.

Grandma said, "He is more powerful than a cow."

From time to time, he would appear outside the window of grandmother's house and look into the room.

Although Grandma knew that he wouldn't do anything bad, she always raised her intimidating fists at him.

He would immediately run away, but would soon run back to the window and look inside again.

Grandma would go out and raise her fists at the dwarf again.

He would run away once more.

This happened many times. It seemed to be a game between Grandma and the dwarf. Grandma was not at all afraid of the dwarf, but nevertheless warned Pika about him saying, "Pika, don't go west!"

Grandma worried that the dwarf would hurt Pika.

The Kite

From time to time, Pika looked out to the west.

Since Pika had returned to Yau Ma Tei, the dwarf had sneaked up to Grandma's window twice. Both times, he had peeked inside and then quickly crept away. He often wandered around on the west side looking at Grandma's house from afar.

Pika and the dwarf always stood watching each other for a very long time from afar.

Then, one day, an event brought Pika and the dwarf together. As usual, they were standing and looking at each other from a distance, when a kite, whose line had been broken, fell from the sky looking like a wounded bird. When it was about 20 meters from the ground, it lingered in the sky, drifting here and there in the wind. The very second the kite landed on the ground between them, Pika and the dwarf ran towards it at high speed. Then they both stood still, looking first at the kite, then at each other, then again at the kite, and then again at each other, as if they were not sure what to do. Neither took a step towards picking it up.

The kite's streamers were fluttering in the breeze. In a nearby tree, a black bird sat watching the scene with its black eyes darting back and forth between the kite, Pika, and the dwarf, while combing its feathers with its beak.

Pika looked away from the dwarf and stepped towards the kite. The dwarf hesitated for a moment and began to walk cautiously up to it as well. Although broken, the kite's line was still very long. Pika found a small wooden stick on the ground to use as a spool and began to wind the line around it. He left a few feet of line free and started running fast across the field, pulling the kite behind him. The wind was just right, and the kite rose higher and higher into the air. The dwarf followed Pika, looking up with delight at the flying kite.

After Pika had been flying the kite for a while, he held out the wooden spool to the dwarf and asked, "Do you want a turn?"

The dwarf stared at Pika and put his hands behind his back.

"Here you go!" said Pika, taking a step forward.

The dwarf took a step back and looked up at him.

"Take it!" Pika again held out the wooden spool.

Still looking at Pika, the dwarf slowly stretched out his hand and grabbed the wooden spool.

"Hurry up," said Pika. "Run quickly."

The dwarf was confused. The kite was losing momentum and was gradually falling from the sky.

"Run!" Pika shouted, and started to run ahead of the dwarf.

Understanding what Pika was trying to tell him, the dwarf ran after him. The kite rose in the air, and the line grew tight.

Pika turned around and watched the dwarf with the kite. When the kite caught the wind, he ran more slowly or even stood still for a while. When the kite began to lose height, he started running fast again. The dwarf had learned well from Pika.

All of a sudden, Pika, his eyes looking up at the sky watching the kite as it flew, fell into a deep hole and disappeared.

In shock on seeing this happen, the dwarf let go of the line and the kite drifted away. He quickly ran over and reached his hands down towards Pika lying in the hole.

Pika looked up at the dwarf. He saw the dwarf's face, eyes, nose and mouth close up, which scared him a little, and he didn't dare hold his hands up.

Stubbornly, the dwarf reached down again.

This time, Pika stretched his hands up and took hold of the dwarf's hands. They felt rough and cold.

The dwarf had a tight grip, which hurt Pika a little. The dwarf was very strong, pulled hard, and at last managed to haul Pika out of the hole.

Meanwhile, the kite had landed on the ground about a hundred meters away. As Pika ran to the kite, the dwarf followed. They picked up the kite and began flying it again in the field.

Grandparents, and many others in Yau Ma Tei had been watching all this with great curiosity. No children ever dared play with the dwarf, and the dwarf didn't play with any of the children. He had only ever exhibited harmful and destructive behaviour.

In the days to come, the people of Yau Ma Tei often saw Pika and the dwarf playing together. The dwarf wanted to please Pika and always followed him and did whatever he asked of him. When Pika took off his shoes and ran barefoot through the field, the dwarf quite happily picked up the shoes and carried them for him.

The Bajiadu Village

Later on, Pika gave the kite to the dwarf. This made the dwarf so happy and he jumped for joy as if he had received a great treasure. He ran all the way home with the kite and tied it to a tree. The wind was not too strong, and the kite floated buoyantly in the sky.

During the day, the dwarf would sit at his door and looked at it with elation. At night, he would get out of bed and admire it again. In the clear moonlight, it was a silent, fluttering shadow.

For several days, the dwarf played with his beloved kite. Whenever it fell to the ground, he succeeded in making it soar up to the sky again.

One afternoon, a strong and blustery wind got up and the kite line broke. The kite didn't lose height, but was caught by the wind and drifted southward. The dwarf chased desperately after it.

The kite eventually landed in a large tree in the neighbouring village of Bajiadu.

Panting heavily, the dwarf rushed up and saw it wrapped helplessly among the branches.

This precious kite, that Pika had given to him!

He climbed up the tree, hugging the trunk tightly. He had always been good at climbing trees, so he quickly reached the top. When he had freed the kite, he screamed with pure joy. As he was about to climb down the tree, he looked down and stiffened in alarm. Standing beneath the tree were more than a dozen Bajiadu children looking angrily up at him.

They held sticks, ropes, bricks, and stones in their hands, as they squinted upwards. Surrounding the tree, they looked like a pack of animals encircling their prey.

They all knew the dwarf. Possibly, they had all been attacked by him at one time or another. So, today was an excellent opportunity for revenge. Even if they hadn't been attacked by him, they thought it would be great fun to torment a fool! They made fun of him, and mocked him shouting hateful and vicious words.

The dwarf looked searchingly into the distance and then upwards, as if he were looking for an escape route in the sky. He stood in the tree, holding a branch in one hand and the kite in the other. The only thing he could think of doing was to stay in the tree and wait for them all to leave and go home.

A bald boy, wearing only shorts, roared to the dwarf, "Dwarf, throw down the kite!"

The dwarf didn't respond.

"Didn't you hear me? Throw down the kite!"

The dwarf still ignored him.

"Didn't you hear me, dwarf? Throw down the kite! Otherwise, you'll be dead meat!" As he said this, the boy patted his belly in a threatening way.

The dwarf looked at the bald boy's face and spat down on him.

The boy wiped off the spit, then swooped forward and flung a hard piece of mud at the dwarf.

The dwarf ducked, but the mud hit his arm. It hurt him and he grimaced and growled, like a wounded beast.

This scared two of the younger children, who turned and ran away. However, the older children didn't run, but all joined in the attack on the dwarf. For some time, they bombarded him with mud, bricks, and stones, most of which smashed noisily against the tree.

Screaming over and over again, the dwarf cowered and tried to protect his head with his arms. The children of Bajiadu were enjoying their attack immensely. Cursing and screaming, they kept searching for more ammunition to throw.

All of a sudden, the dwarf stopped protecting his head with his hands, straightened up his neck and body, and furiously scowled down at them. This bewildered the children. Grabbing the kite and looking at the bald boy, the dwarf unexpectedly sprang from the tree and jumped right onto him. The other children ran away.

The dwarf landed awkwardly and it took him a while to stand up. This gave the bald boy the opportunity to rush over and heave his body on top of him, crushing him on the ground.

He shouted to the other children, "Come here! Come over here!"

The fleeing children turned around, saw the bald boy lying on top of the dwarf, ran back, and all pounced in a heap and helped him pin the dwarf down.

The dwarf struggled to look up, and the bald boy quickly pushed his head down with both his hand until his mouth was pressed into the filthy mud.

A boy with a flat nose tried to seize the kite, but the dwarf grasped onto it tightly. The boy then tried to prise open the dwarf's hand, but couldn't do it. He got so angry that he grabbed at the kite and it tore in half. The dwarf whimpered miserably, and looked like a desperate young beast.

Pika had seen the dwarf chase the kite to Bajiadu. When he

discovered he had not returned, he suspected that he may have been attacked by the children of Bajiadu. Pike rushed to band together a group of children from Yau Ma Tei, and he led them to Bajiadu.

When they found the dwarf an hour later, the children of Bajiadu had already left. The dwarf was tied to the tree. His head was drooping down as if he were dead, but he still held the remains of the kite in his hand ...

A Crazy Night

It was the middle of the night and everyone was fast asleep. The dwarf awoke and sat up in his bed. He decided to sneak out, so instead of leaving through the door, he pushed open the window behind his bed, put both hands on the windowsill, and quietly jumped out. He went straight to Bajiadu.

The night was damp, dewdrops had formed on the blades of grass on the roadside, and the dwarf walked barefoot and shirtless in the dim moonlight. The moon, intermittently overcast by clouds, seemed to have no energy, as if it were tired and bored and wanted to go home, thinking, *Everyone is sleeping soundly, so why should I hang around in the sky?*

The dwarf seemed to be even shorter in the moonlight. As he walked through the fields, the crops on either side were taller than he was, and so, if anyone had been standing in the fields they wouldn't have been able to see him. Unlike other children, the dwarf was not afraid of the night and in fact, preferred to roam about in the dark.

On this particular night, he was the only person around.

He wandered through fields, along the riverbank, and into a cemetery. He walked from tomb to tomb and occasionally sat down on a grave to watch the blue fireflies fluttering on the weeds. He lay down for a few moments in an abandoned melon shed, and again under a tall tree by the river, and felt as comfortable as if he were in his own bed.

For most of the journey, he meandered along slowly. However, when his wounds became painful, he started running quickly towards Bajiadu.

All the people in Bajiadu slept like dead pigs.

At last he arrived in Bajiadu, the first thing he came to was the huge tree that he had been tied up to. Looking up at its branches, he vividly recalled the attack by the children of Bajiadu.

He walked along the lane through the village. As he went, he opened the gates of every pig pen and sheep pen he came to and let all the pigs and sheep out. He did the same to the duck pens and the chicken coops. In addition to releasing the animals, he caused a lot more damage along the way. He flung a sheepskin into a soy sauce tank, threw garments hanging on a clothesline into a drain, uprooted flowers, unbridled a donkey, hurled a pair of shoes he found outside a house into a toilet, broke a fish tank and left the fish lying on the ground, took the valve off a bicycle tyre, climbed over a garden fence and dumped a large bundle of corn he found hanging on the wall into a water tank ... and much more ...

He managed to sneak into three separate kitchens, chucked all the rice out of the rice bowls, shook up bottles of soy sauce, and sprayed the soy sauce all over the walls. Each time, he sneered and spat onto the ground.

In front of one home he saw a parked tractor. He found the toolbox, and under the light of the moon he unscrewed all the nuts and bolts, removed as many parts as possible from the tractor, and threw them all away.

The dwarf did all these bad deeds calmly and with no emotion.

He went to the wharf on the riverbank and tossed away the stones that were used for steps. He grew tired and sat on the stones for a while. When a white fish jumped out of the water, he couldn't help but clap his hands with satisfaction.

It was time he went home. All the pigs and sheep of Bajiadu had made their way into the vegetable garden and the cropland, and were happily eating everything they could find in the moonlight. They were very excited, and had never before experienced such wonderful nightlife! As if they had been given an order not to "oink" or "baa," they munched away quietly, enjoying their fantastic midnight feast!

After they had eaten everything, the land was all churned up, muddy, and bare.

The chickens and ducks waddled and flew around in chaos.

The dwarf saw a sickle that had been left outside. He picked it up and saw how brightly it shone in the moonlight. He then walked to the lane that ran through the middle of the village. On either side of the lane were rows of sunflowers. Their heads were slightly bowed under the night sky. He slashed at them with the blade of the sickle and watched their heads tumble off. He strolled along, chopping at the rest of the sunflowers until all the heads were lying sadly on the ground. The dwarf thought that the tall sunflower stalks without heads looked quite ridiculous.

By the time the dwarf arrived back at Yau Ma Tei, the sun had come up and the new day was dawning.

In Hiding

As daylight broke, the world that the people of Bajiadu witnessed could be described in one word: catastrophic.

The pigs and sheep that had eaten too much food were sleeping comfortably in the morning breeze.

What a mess!

"Who did this?"

"Who did this?"

Fraught with anger, everyone screamed out these questions again and again.

After a while, the dwarf came to mind. Last night, they had heard that the children of the village had beaten up the dwarf and tied him to a big tree.

"The dwarf!"

"It must be the dwarf!"

Everyone quickly gathered together.

"Let him go to hell!"

"Kill him!"

Several of the women were crying after seeing that the vegetable garden and their crops had been completely destroyed.

A large crowd of village people got together, and carrying all kinds of weapons, rushed to Yau Ma Tei.

Pika and Huaer were looking for a pond where they could catch fish. They saw the angry mob in the distance and heard them cursing the dwarf.

Pika said to Huaer, "Quick! We need to hide the dwarf!"

72

He ran all the way to Yau Ma Tei Primary School and to the house on the west side.

The dwarf, exhausted after last night, was sleeping soundly.

Pika shook him fiercely, waking him up, "Quick! You need to hide! The people of Bajiadu are coming here to kill you!"

Confused, the dwarf looked drowsily up at Pika.

"Don't you understand? Many, many people from Bajiadu are on their way here! They are going to kill you! You must hide at once!"

The dwarf's mother Mrs. Silly seemed to understand a little bit about what was going on, and stood in fear against the wall in the corner.

The dwarf finally grasped the full meaning of the situation. He leapt out of bed and look helplessly at Pika.

Pika opened the back window, jumped out, and beckoned to the dwarf to follow him. The dwarf jumped out, and the two boys ran behind the house to the bamboo forest.

The people of Bajiadu had rushed straight onto the campus of Yau Ma Tei Primary School.

Pika thought that if the dwarf stayed in the bamboo forest, he would be easily found.

He said to the dwarf, "Follow me!"

He dashed towards the back of the toilet, and from there into another part of the bamboo forest, and from there to the back of Grandpa's house.

People were running all over campus cursing the dwarf, and they spread out in all directions in search of him.

Pika knew that the angry mobs might find them at the back

of Grandpa's house, so he wanted to take the dwarf and hide him inside the house. But he didn't have time to take him round to the front because a couple of Bajiadu villagers were already walking in through the front door. He pushed the back window, but it was locked from inside and couldn't be opened. He banged on the window to ask the people inside to open it, but there was no one in the room - his grandparents and aunt had gone outside to watch what was going on. He grabbed a brick from the ground, smashed the glass, put his hand inside, pulled on the latch, opened the window, jumped into the room, and then let the dwarf into the house.

"Be quick! Hide under the bed!" Pika held up the overhanging sheets and shoved the dwarf under the bed. The dwarf obediently did as he was told.

"You must never come out unless I tell you to!" declared Pika, as he pulled the sheets down.

Pika went out into the yard. The people of Yau Ma Tei and of Bajiadu were swarming all over campus.

The Bajiadu people cursed and screamed ... they had good reason to. They rushed into the house on the west side, and smashed everything in sight. Bottles of oil and soy sauce were broken, and their contents spilled onto the floor. Mrs. Silly tried to protect her things, but she was stopped by a strong man who pushed her so hard that she slammed to the ground.

The woman started to cry, and the man shouted at her, "Don't you dare cry! Your son is a jerk!"

Then they smashed more things until there was nothing else left to destroy. They bashed the wall in anger, and brutally kicked the dwarf's mother as they left the house.

The people of Yau Ma Tei looked on and waited to see what

74

would happen next.

The people of Bajiadu still had much resentment to vent, and they were determined to catch the dwarf.

"When we catch him, we must kill him!" they swore.

"Dwarf, come out! Show yourself!" they shouted as they searched the campus.

Grandma whispered to Pika, "Have you seen the dwarf?"

Pika shook his head.

Grandma was worried and said, "I don't know where he is."

Someone looked suspiciously into Grandpa's yard.

This made Grandma angry and she declared, "He's not here!"

But the man continued looking into the yard.

The two doors to the courtyard were half open. Grandma reached forward and opened them, saying, "Look! Look! There's nobody here!"

The man then entered the yard. This made Pika very nervous. As the man looked around, Pika felt his heart thumping. The man glanced inside the room and at last walked out of the yard.

As he left, he said to Grandma, "I was only looking."

The people of Yau Ma Tei watched in silence as the people of Bajiadu continued their search.

They refused to leave, and some of them sat on the ground and said, "We're staying here! We don't believe he can hide forever!"

The man from Bajiadu beat the dwarf's mother up again. Some of the Yau Ma Tei villagers were now very fed up and began to curse impatiently. The atmosphere on the school campus grew more and more tense as groups gathered together there.

Grandpa gave the situation much thought and went to find the leader of the Bajiadu people.

He said to him, "You had better leave. Don't forget, this is our community. As the old saying goes, if you want to beat a dog, you have to consider its owner. Although the dwarf is a fool, he is also a villager of Yau Ma Tei. He is one of us. Don't resent us. If you cling to resentment, it's you that will suffer. Besides, you are not being reasonable. Remember, your children beat him. They hurt him badly and tied him to a tree! He is a fool, so how can you treat him like this? Accept defeat. Forget about it ..."

In matters of conflict, Grandpa was someone who was especially sensible and always managed to convince people to see reason.

The Bajiadu leader listened and nodded his head. Then he walked to his people and said something.

After a while, he went and shook hands with Grandpa, "Sir! I have thought about what you have said."

He turned around and shouted to the people of Bajiadu, "Everyone go home, now. There is no end to this! But that dwarf had better remember ... even if he buries himself in a deep hole, we will dig him out! We know you're hiding! You have escaped from us today, but you can't hide from us forever! Let's go home!"

And with that, the people of Bajiadu left.

But the people of Yau Ma Tei were still annoyed.

Grandpa smiled calmly, "The dwarf has done serious damage to their homes and it is reasonable for them to be angry."

They agreed with Grandpa, "The dwarf should be punished! He is the scourge of Yau Ma Tei. Maybe we should kill him!"

Grandpa smiled again, "It's a life you're talking about. If you take a life, you must pay for it. If you kill him, you will have to go to jail!"

Someone asked, "Where is the dwarf hiding?"

Nobody had any idea.

Pika ran into the house, lifted up the sheets and cried, "They have gone. Come out."

But there was no movement.

Pika squatted down and looked under the bed, only to see that the dwarf was sleeping ...

The Screams of Mrs. Silly

One night, a week later, everyone in Yau Ma Tei awoke to the screams of the dwarf's mother!

"Help!"

Although she spoke in her strange accent, they clearly heard what she was yelling, and all ran to the Yau Ma Tei Primary School campus.

Grandpa, Grandma, Aunt and Pika reached the west side of the campus first. The woman was holding her head and running desperately towards them.

"Help!" Her shouts, in the quiet of the night, sounded particularly piercing.

Grandpa and Grandma kept asking, "What's the matter? What's the matter?"

But the distressed woman only shouted, "Help!"

In the moonlight, Grandpa, Grandma, Aunt and Pika saw a short black shadow holding a stick running towards them. They instantly recognised him: the dwarf!

By now, many other people had arrived on the scene.

Mrs. Silly ran into the crowd, still shouting, "Help!" Her voice was softer now, but trembling.

The dwarf stood there, grasping the stick. His icy and menacing glare was like the glare of a jungle beast waiting to attack, and made the hearts of both the adults and the children constrict with alarm.

Someone shone their lantern onto the dwarf's mother. They saw her head had been bashed in, and blood flowed down her face.

She sat on the ground, "Help!" But it almost seemed as if she were talking to herself.

Someone squatted down beside her and asked, "Why is he hitting you?"

The frightened woman just kept repeating, "Help! Help!"

After a while, some of the people figured out that there was probably no food in the dwarf's house. When he had woken up in the middle of the night, he had been hungry. He had asked his mother for something to eat, but there had been no food. He had grabbed a stick and severely beaten his own mother.

Pika looked into the dwarf's eyes, and couldn't help but grasp hold of his aunt's hand.

Grandma went home and fetched some food.

She gave it to the woman, saying, "Don't scream so loudly again in the middle of the night."

In the light of the lantern, Pika saw her bloody face and gripped his aunt's hand even more tightly.

The crowd gradually dispersed.

As they walked home, Grandma said to Pika, "Stay away from the dwarf in future!"

This time, Pika nodded and agreed.

Dwarf, where are you?

Thinking about how the dwarf had destroyed Bajiadu, the bloody face of his mother, and his icy cold glare under the moonlight, Pika was scared that the dwarf's face might suddenly appear at the window. He shut it quickly.

Grandma said, "It's such a hot day! Why did you close the window!" She walked over and opened it.

Pika closed it again.

Aunt ordered, "Open the window!"

Pika decided that he was never again going to the house on the west side.

That afternoon, Pika and Huaer were in the field chasing a brown cockroach, when the dwarf ran towards them.

Huaer said, "The dwarf is coming!"

Pika turned around and looked at the dwarf, and said softly to Huaer, "Let's go."

Confused, the dwarf stood there, looking at the back of Pika and Huaer as they walked away.

When the dwarf next appeared at Pika's grandmother's window, Grandma raised her fists at him. But this time, it was quite obvious she wasn't playing a game, but was very serious and giving him a harsh warning to go away.

In the days that followed, the dwarf no longer appeared at

the window.

One day, Pika went to look at the boats on the river. He noticed the dwarf walking along the riverbank to the north. He thought to himself, *He's going northwards! Where is he going?*

Just then, the dwarf turned around and saw Pika. He started watching him, but Pika ignored him and turned away to look again at the river. The dwarf hesitated for a second, then turned around and continued to walk to the north.

Pika wanted to ask him, *Where are you going? Are you going home? Your home is not in that direction! Come back!*

Instead, Pika watched him go farther and farther, and farther and farther ...

That night, the dwarf's mother knocked on Grandma's door and said, "My son is lost."

Grandma comforted her, "Go back to bed. I'm sure he'll be back in the morning."

The woman declared, "He said he was going to find his father."

"Nonsense! He doesn't know where his father is. And even if he does, he doesn't know how to get there! Go back to sleep and look for him tomorrow."

Pika had woken up and heard the conversation between the two women. He was a little upset.

Grandma asked Grandpa, "Do you think he's lost?"

"It is quite normal for a fool to get lost."

Grandma gave a heavy sigh.

Days went by, and nobody saw the dwarf.

Grandpa got together a dozen people, divided them into teams, and went looking in all directions. But they found no trace of the dwarf.

Pika was very unhappy and rarely spoke. Grandpa asked him what was wrong, and he wouldn't say. Grandma asked him what was wrong, and he wouldn't say.

Aunt asked why, and Pika cried, "I saw him going north one day. I didn't call to him. If I had called to him, he would have turned back."

Aunt comforted him, "That is not necessarily true. He said he was going to find his father, therefore no one could have made him come back."

Pika stubbornly replied, "If I had called to him, he definitely would have come back."

The dwarf never did return.

And now Pika was going back to Beijing ... school was soon to begin.

Pika asked Grandpa to make him a kite. The day before he left, he launched the kite into the sky and then tied the line to the tree in front of the dwarf's house ...

The Field of Wormwoods

Yau Ma Tei Primary School was surrounded by water and stood by itself on a very small island.

Mrs. Qin's little thatched cottage was squeezed tightly into the northwest corner, and looked like it could fall into the river at any moment. The cottage was drab, and a shabby blot on the landscape that destroyed the harmony and beauty of Yau Ma Tei Primary School.

The local government wanted to evict Mrs. Qin from the land, but ten years had passed and they still hadn't succeeded.

Mrs. Qin firmly believed that the land belonged to her.

And maybe it did!

Mrs. Qin's husband was called Qin da. He and Mrs. Qin had no previous connection to the land, however, after thinking about it for many years, they finally purchased it in early 1948. They became obsessed with their land and thought of nothing else. They had no regard as to whether it was day or night, cloudy or sunny, hot or cold. They also put aside their everyday needs, such as wearing a new coat to keep out the wind and cold, eating a slice of watermelon to quench their thirst, eating meat to satisfy their hunger, and even sleeping. Gradually, they became numb to their discomfort. For example, they felt no pain if they cut their fingers with a sickle, if their backs ached, or if their bare feet cracked and bled during the cold winter.

When Qin Da was alive, people would say of him, "That man is so stingy and mean. If he got pierced with an awl, he wouldn't shed a single drop of blood! If he fell down on the ground, he would take the time to grab hold of a handful of mud before getting up!"

The only thing that made the childless couple happy was to dream about their land. It had good Feng Shui; the wheat seedlings trembled in the spring breeze as lovely as a child, and the wheat glistened like gold under the May sunshine.

After years of hard work, in the middle of their land they built a thatched cottage. From that moment, their tired eyes focused solely on the development of the land. One year, spring came earlier than ever before. It was only February when the wind became warm. Day by day, the wheat grew and grew, until soon the soil was completely covered by a field of green. The field was so large that when you were outside and a warm breeze began to blow, it felt like you were standing in the middle of a vast sea of rippling green waves.

One day, while working in the field, Qin Da died, so sadly didn't live to see the May harvest.

When the villagers put him in his coffin, they remarked, "We've carried a lot of dead people, but we've never carried anyone as light as this one before!"

Mrs. Qin did live to see the next harvest, but by that time the government had declared that land was no longer allowed to be owned by individuals.

As the weather continued to improve, the people of Yau Ma Tei came up with a variety of new ideas for their village.

One of the most popular ideas was to build a school where the children could be educated. Without exception, when choosing the location for the school, the local government officials and the villagers all cast their eyes on the lovely piece of land that was surrounded by water. And so, some people were sent to pull up weeds by the beach, and others went to ask Mrs. Qin to move. However, when she saw a dozen boats all piled high with thatch moor alongside the river, she refused to go.

The local government kindly built her a house elsewhere on a small piece of land. But Mrs. Qin didn't want it. She sat stubbornly on the ground and yelled, "Come on! Just try and move me! I won't leave here until I'm dead."

The officials were patient and reasoned with her, "Running a school is a great undertaking that will benefit future generations."

Mrs. Qin closed her eyes and said, "I have no future generations." It really didn't make any sense to her.

The school was to be built in the autumn. The people of Yau Ma Tei were helpless. An official came and asked why the school had not yet been started. The villagers explained.

The official said, "This is outrageous! We must get her out of here!"

The local government had to think of a solution.

That day, all the villagers got together. Some harvested the wheat, and some climbed onto the thatched cottage and started to tear it down. Mrs. Qin was carried away by several militiamen. She fought as hard as she could, but they were too strong for her.

She could only cry, "I want my land! My land."

She spat at the men and shouted to the people, "Help! Help!" But no one responded.

Mrs. Qin was forced to move into the new house that had been built for her. She banged against the doors and windows and shouted abuse.

The militiamen shouted, "If you make any more noise, you'll be tied up and sent away." Then they left her alone.

When Mrs. Qin finally got out of the house by breaking the window and ran back to the land, her cottage had already been gone, and all the wheat had been harvested. It was piled high and shone in the sun. The ground was covered with white lines of lime and piles of wood, and the foundations for the school had already been excavated. Everything had changed.

Her eyes glazed in thought and she sat on the ground until dark. She decided to take legal action and to sue. She brought her accusation to the village, then the district, then the county, over and over again. Her hair began to turn white, and she became stooped with age.People tried to reason with her, but she wouldn't listen to them. They banged their fists on the table in an attempt to frighten her, but she just lay at their feet, "Go ahead and tie me up! Tie me up and throw me in jail!"

Village business of course could only be carried out according to the will of the people of Yau Ma Tei. Yau Ma Tei Primary School had been built and was the most beautiful school for miles around. Every morning, the children arrived at the school from all directions, singing and dancing happily. Every morning, a bright red flag was raised to the top of the flagpole, where it fluttered gently in the wind.

The sound of young voices reading could be heard coming from the school. The people of Yau Ma Tei had never before heard the pure, vibrant chorus of children reading. Boats passing by would slow down and listen. And as the sound spread to the fields, the villagers would feel an inexplicable excitement in their hearts. Sometimes, a farmer working on the land with his hoe could also be heard singing hoarsely and vigorously as he went about his work!

Mrs. Qin regularly went along to the school to complain. Again and again she told the schoolchildren, "This land belongs to me!"

The children just smiled. Some of them thought she was strange and were a little afraid of her. When they saw hatred in her expression, they quickly ran to the safety of the campus.

There were many nights when the teachers watched Mrs. Qin walking around the school grounds like a ghost.

Government officials at all levels were constantly annoyed with her, but there was nothing they could do. In the end, they had to make some concessions. So they all came to an agreement. On a small piece of land by the Yau Ma Tei Primary School, the government built her a little straw house.

Two

By the time Sangsang came to Yau Ma Tei Primary School with his father, Mrs. Qin had lived in her house in the northwest corner for several years.

Walking around the campus one day, Sangsang came upon Mrs. Qin's house. Immediately, he was surrounded by the strong and bitter smell of wormwood. He saw that the patch of wormwood in front of him surrounded the little straw house. The wind was blowing the wormwood leaves up and down and around. The colours on the front and back of a wormwood leaf are different. The front is a greyish green, while the underside has fuzzy hairs and is much paler, almost a silvery white. Therefore, as all the different shades blended together, they twinkled as they blew in the wind. Wormwood doesn't grow very tall, but its stems are upright and erect, like a pen. Nevertheless, the foliage is loose and formless, fine, and dense.

Sangsang made his way between the wormwood shrubs and came to the door of the house. A light shone inside. Sangsang peered in trying to see who and what was inside. He saw an old stooped woman amid some simple furniture.

Sansang wondered, Is she alone? He looked back at the empty space around him and felt lonely. So he very much wanted to go in and meet the old woman.

Mrs. Qin had a feeling there was someone outside her door, and she went to have a look.

The sun was shining in the sky. When Mrs. Qin appeared before him in the sunlight, she left a deep impression on Sangsang that he would never forget. She was tall and well-proportioned, but her back was bent and hunched. She was clean and tidy, and on her small feet wore black shoes embroidered with golden flowers. She leaned on a cane for support, and her white hair fluttered slightly in the wind.

Strangely, as if he knew her, Sangsang said, "Grandma!"

Mrs. Qin looked quizzically at Sangsang. The children here never call her grandmother, they all called her "old woman" or "Mrs. Qin." She reached out and touched Sangsang's head. She had never made such an intimate gesture before.

She asked, "Who are you?"

"I am Sangsang."

"How come I've never met you?"

"I just moved here."

"Where do you live?"

"I live here, on this campus, just like you."

Mrs. Qin was puzzled.

Sangsang said, "My dad just transferred here as the new headmaster."

"Oh!" Mrs. Qin nodded, "Yes, there is a new headmaster."

Sangsang reached down and touched the wormwood beside her.

Mrs. Qin asked, "Do you know what this is? It's wormwood."

"Why is there so much of it?"

"Wormwood is clean and it has a medicinal smell. In summer, there are no mosquitoes or flies here."

"But crops should grow here!"

"Crops? What crops?"

"Something like wheat."

"Originally, this land was full of wheat. But, it's no longer cultivated here. Only wormwood grows here now."

At their first meeting, Sangsang and Mrs. Qin talked a lot.

Mrs. Qin's mind was preoccupied as always with the subject of the land, and she pointed with her stick and declared,

"This entire land belongs to me! What a fine piece of land!"

Sangsang stayed chatting to Mrs. Qin until he heard his

mother calling him from the distance.

Later on, Sangsang began hearing from the adults that Mrs. Qin was a very hateful old woman. They spoke about how they all knew she could clearly see the path that went around the school garden. But, she would pretend it wasn't there and would walk straight through it with her cane, trampling down many of the plants as she went.

In the autumn, if people didn't keep an eye on her, she would pick the melons or herbs from the school garden, and instead of eating them herself, would throw them into the river. She also kept flocks of chickens, ducks, and geese, and let them run around the school grounds. The school built a fence around the garden, but the sneaky birds would still get in and eat the young plants and fresh fruit. One day, Mrs. Qin lost a chicken and insisted that the children had frightened it away. The chicken hid in the grass and was eaten by a weasel. She argued with the school authorities, who finally paid her a little money in compensation.

One day, during breaktime, Sangsang was going to take Shu to see the wormwoods.

Tuhe, who was playing nearby, advised, "Don't go! Mrs. Qin will hit you on the head with her cane."

Sangsang didn't believe him and went alone.

Some little first grade girls were hiding in the wormwoods and peeking into the little house. When they saw Mrs. Qin coming towards them they were extremely frightened and ran away fast like rabbits. Mrs. Qin looked down at the wormwoods that had been trampled down and angrily thumped the ground with her cane.

But Sangsang was not afraid and went right up to Mrs. Qin.

When they heard Sangsang calling her Grandma and ask her for a wormwood, the little girls admired him and thought he was very brave. Sangsang was confused, *Why did people think she so scary?*

Principal Sang Qiao had a poor impression of Mrs. Qin. One day as he walked around inspecting his campus, he came upon the wormwoods and the little straw house. He felt troubled. After listening to what the teachers said about Mrs. Qin, he thought it was absolutely unreasonable that an old woman who had nothing to do with Yau Ma Tei Primary School should be allowed to live on the school grounds. He walked through the wormwoods and up to the house. Mrs. Qin was sitting in the sun at her door.

"Hello!" Sang Qiao said.

Mrs. Qin looked at Sang Qiao and did not answer.

After looking around at the little house, he felt that this good piece of land in the northwest corner of Yau Ma Tei should belong to his school, and not to Mrs. Qin. He felt profoundly indignant.

Mrs. Qin asked, "Who are you? You look like a bad guy!"

Sang Qiao thought the old woman was excessively rude, then said seriously, "I am Sang Qiao."

"I don't know you."

"I am the headmaster!"

Mrs. Qin stood up and said, "Do you want to drive me away from my home?"

"I didn't say that."

"All this land belongs to me!"

Sang Qiao thought she was ridiculous. These days, land was no longer privately owned. He didn't respond, and left the wormwoods. But when he came to the southern end of the land, he looked back at the wormwoods and felt Yau Ma Tei Primary School was fragmented and incomplete.

In the spring, Sang Qiao got the whole school together to collect chinabery seeds. He wanted to plant them all over the campus. The chinaberry was the most popular local tree. In spring, when in full bloom, the delicate lilac flowers looked like a pale blue cloud in the distance. Chinaberry didn't attract worms because it was bitter. In summer, it could be used in toilets to eliminate the smell and the maggots. Chinaberry was not only beautiful and clean, but also the source of the most beneficial wood in the area. Sang Qiao had looked in all the classrooms and found that many of the desks were old and broken. When considering which field to use as a nursery for growing the chinaberry trees, Sang Qiao thought of the wormwood fields in the northwest. To avoid conflict with Mrs. Qin, he asked several teachers who had been teaching for a long time at Yau Ma Tei Primary School how much of the land in the northwest corner had been given to Mrs. Qin. He had a suspicion that she could not have been given so much land. The teacher's completely confirmed his suspicion. And so, he decided to use that land for the nursery.

On the day they began work on the nursery, Sang Qiao wanted to go and say hello to Mrs. Qin. However, she had gone into town to sell some chickens. After a while, when she still hadn't returned, Sang Qiao said to the teachers and students, "We don't have to wait. Pull up the weeds."

The wormwoods were pulled up in no time. Next, shovels turned over the soil. Sang Qiao himself then scattered the chinaberry seeds, covered them over with earth, and poured water over them. By the time Mrs. Qin came back from the town, everyone had already gone and she was left looking at the nursery. She stood there for a long time, and then poked some holes in the ground with her cane.

She shouted, "This is my land! Mine! "

A few days later, the chinaberry saplings poked their heads timidly out of the ground and swayed gaily in the cool wind. This image reminded Mrs. Qin of when her wheat seedlings had also swayed happily in the breeze in the spring. To her, It looked like the chinaberry saplings were winking and laughing at her, and she wanted to whip them right away from her land.

In the warm spring air, the chinaberry saplings continued to grow. Mrs. Qin imagined that they would soon spread like crazy throughout the land until they occupied all the earth! When she thought about this, she wanted to roll around in the nursery and crush those heartless trees. However, she didn't do that right away. But one day, a group of students, with their teacher's permission, began to chase her flock of chickens. They flew off and laid their eggs where she couldn't find them. It was in that moment that she decided to destroy the nursery.

There was no one around.

Mrs. Qin, normally a clean and tidy person, unexpectedly lay down on the ground and rolled and rolled from east to west of the nursery like a naughty child.

Sangsang was coming from the wormwoods behind her little hut, but Mrs. Qin didn't see him. Sangsang watched her rolling all over the nursery, and grinned.

Mrs. Qin looked like a quilted bundle as she rolled. She

was so focused, that a couple of times she rolled right out of the nursery. She corrected her position and continued to roll again from east to west, and from west to east. Her eyes were closed and she muttered, "The land is mine, so I can do anything I want!"

The saplings were pliant so that Mrs. Qin couldn't break them. She flattened them onto the ground as she rolled over them, but a few moments later they slowly sprung up again.

When Sangsang saw Mrs. Qin roll outside the nursery boundary once more, he laughed, jumped up and down, clapped his hands, and said, "Grandma rolled out!"

Mrs. Qin stopped rolling and looked up at Sangsang.

Sangsang approached her.

Mrs. Qin asked, "Could you please not tell your father?"

Sangsang thought for a moment and then nodded.

Sangsang, who was often said by his father to "have no sense of right and wrong," suddenly felt that by comparison Mrs. Qin was very reasonable.

Three

Sang Qiao wanted his kingdom to be perfect, and each day his grand ideas for expansion and development grew stronger. He planted willows all along the river so that soon they replaced the wormwoods behind Mrs. Qin's little house. As soon as they were planted, Mrs. Qin pulled them up. However, each time she did this Sang Qiao sent people to plant them again. Mrs. Qin was involved in a fight against her biggest enemy-Yau Ma Tei Primary School-which was trying to drive her out step by step.

Despite being alone, she didn't feel sad or powerless. She

had her "comrades-in-arms" -her chickens, ducks and geese to help her. Every morning, she drove them with a willow branch into the school's office and classrooms.

The chickens pooped all over the campus, and in the middle of a lesson would run into the classrooms, clucking and cackling as they darted around between the children's legs. Under the watchful eyes of their teachers, the children were silent in class, and the chickens enjoyed the quiet environment and felt relaxed and comfortable. They pecked at the plaster on the walls, sat at the children's feet, unfurled their feathers, and washed themselves in the dusty earth.

The ducks would also run into the classrooms, waddling and searching for food on the ground with their bills. They also pooped all over the place and were really smelly. The children held their noses and didn't dare make a sound. One of the girls was called up to the front to read from her book. Her voice was so nasally because she didn't want to breathe in through her nose. "What's wrong with your nose?" asked the teacher. Then, all the children laughed at the teacher because she also sounded like someone with severe sinusitis!

The two geese ate grass by the office gate, and when they were in high spirits, they honked loudly and sounded like a great ship blasting its horn out at sea.

At noon, when the children went home for lunch, the chickens, ducks and geese would go into the classrooms. When the children came back to school, they found piles of excrement on the desktops and stools. Once, a child was secretly playing with something in his desk drawer when he touched an egg.

Forgetting himself completely, he cried out, "An egg!"

The other children all turned around and cried out together, "Egg! An egg!"

They only quietened down when the teacher banged on the blackboard with the eraser. The boy who had found the egg was punished. He was made to stand in class awkwardly holding the egg in his hand.

After class, he rushed out of the classroom and shouted, "Damn old woman!" Then he threw the egg as hard as he could. It flew across the pond, hit a tree, smashed, and spilled its bright yellow yolk all down the tree trunk.

Sang Qiao sent a teacher to tell Mrs. Qin not to let the chickens, ducks and geese walk around campus anymore.

Mrs. Qin said, "They aren't human! How can I possibly control them?"

Yau Ma Tei Primary School spent money on buying bundles of reeds and used them to build a high fence to keep the fowl from coming onto the school grounds. The chickens, ducks and geese, who had been used to roaming wherever they like, didn't like their loss of freedom. They flew and jumped around noisily, depriving Mrs. Qin of any peace and quiet. Mrs. Qin viewed the fence as if it were an ugly barricade of barbed wire.

One day, two third grade students were fighting. One of them beat the other to the ground, then, realising that he was badly hurt, fled in a panic. His opponent jumped up, grabbed a brick and ran after him, chasing him right up to the fence. Turning round, the boy in front saw his enemy racing menacingly towards him, so he hurled himself at the fence like a wild boar and ran straight through it.

There was now a big gaping hole in the fence!

That day, the town secretary had invited dozens of primary school principals to come to Yau Ma Tei Primary School to inspect their work. When the bell rang, the secretary divided the principals into several groups and Sang Qiao and the others teachers took them around to each classroom. Everything was going well, and Sang Qiao thought to himself that it was a good thing he had built the fence a few days before.

Sang Qiao was accompanied by the secretary. They went to the fourth grade Chinese class. The teacher, Wen Youju, was both a kind and serious instructor.

Under Sang Qiao's management, the school was run with meticulous care and attention to detail.

The classroom discipline seemed a little rigid. When the secretary and Sang Qiao entered the room, the well-trained children sat and didn't say a word, just if no one had come in. Afraid to make a sound, the secretary sat down as quietly as he could. The blackboard was spotlessly clean and looked as if it had just been washed. Wen Youju raised her slender hand and wrote down the title of the lesson on the blackboard. Her handwriting was very neat.

She began the lesson. She didn't teach with energy, but was not boring either. Her voice was as gentle as the breeze, but she spoke with a passion that held the attention of the lively children and transported them to another world. The children forget about their everyday activities like chasing around in mud, catching birds with nets in the bamboo forest, watching the dogs running around the fields, throwing stones in the river, and playing shuttlecock. Their Chinese teacher's gentle lyrical voice was music to their ears.

As a result of Sang Qiao's exceptional leadership, almost every classroom exhibited a unique charm all of its own.

Nobody realised it yet, but Mrs. Qin's army had already marched through the big hole in the fence and was on its way to the school. The chickens, ducks and geese, who had now been fenced in for several days, were very excited at making their escape. When they got through the hole and onto the land where they used to roam freely, they scurried forward flapping their wings madly leaving a trail of dust behind them, and causing the fallen leaves to scatter everywhere.

The sounds of their feet scuttling over the ground and their wings beating against the air resonated like the autumn wind sweeping through a barren forest.

On hearing the cackle of a goose, Sang Qiao glanced up and saw a flock of chickens, ducks and geese waddling towards the school. Some of the chickens stopped at the door of Wen Youju's classroom. Sang Qiao glared at them in an attempt to make them go away, but knew it wouldn't work because they were only chickens and not his students! They were now on the threshold. One of them flapped its wings, tilted its head, and looked into the room. The classroom was as still as a mill pond, and the only sound that could be heard was the whisper of Ms Wen's voice.

After a few moments, the chickens entered the classroom. They saw it as a special place to forage. There were no bugs, but tiny crumbs that children dropped to the ground. The students sat very still, and their legs and the legs of the tables and benches were static, and so in the eyes of the chickens, it didn't seem all that different from the forests they wandered about in.

A green-tailed rooster wasn't interested in foraging. He spent his time trying to woo one of the hens. The hen seemed to be accustomed to his repeated and annoying advances and simply dodged away from him and went back to her own foraging.

When a chicken came up close to his feet, Sang Qiao kicked it with his foot in an attempt to frighten it out of the classroom. But the chicken merely moved aside and took no notice.

Sang Qiao looked over at the secretary, who was frowning at a hen that was about to jump onto a child's stool. He felt anxious and was afraid that it would start flapping its wings and fly onto the child's lap. Thankfully, his fears were dispelled when the hen was distracted by the rooster sneaking up behind her and causing her to strut quickly away.

All the children had noticed the chickens by now. However, not wanting to disappoint Sang Qiao, they resolutely ignored them.

Although Ms Wen had seen the chickens the moment they stepped into the classroom, she continued to try to teach as if nothing unusual had happened. Nevertheless, Sang Qiao could see that she was agitated. Ms Wen could see the image of the chickens in her mind as she lectured, and her usual calm voice began to falter with unease.

Outside, the energetic quacking of some ducks disrupted the general silence on campus.

By now, some of the children could not help looking out of the window.

It was about thirty-five minutes after class had begun, when a hen wandered down the aisle wildly flapping her wings. The floor of the classroom was just bare earth, not concrete or brick. Because the children constantly trampled over it, it was always covered with a thick layer of dust, even after cleaning. The hen's flapping wings stirred up the dust, which blew through the air like a whirlwind of yellow ash. Few girls sat next to the window and when they saw the ash, the girls bent their heads and covered their faces with their arms. One of the boys, who wanted to help the girls avoid the dust, gave the hen a hard kick. It squawked and ran madly around the classroom. Ms Wen gave the boy a reproachful look.

Even though Ms Wen temporarily managed to calm her students down, they didn't really take much notice because all they could think about was what might happen next. They all waited for the next antic to be performed by the chicken.

The usual peaceful atmosphere of the classroom had virtually disappeared.

A chicken pooped just an inch or two in front of the toes of one of the schoolmasters.

About forty minutes into the lesson, a hen stopped next to a boy's leg. She looked at his pale skin that was exposed by a small hole in his trousers. What is this? thought the chicken as she pecked at the skin with her beak. The boy shrieked, turning the quiet classroom into uproar.

Ms Wen yelled, "Get the chickens out of here!" But before she had even finished speaking, the children had already jumped into action.

The chaos began! All sorts of things danced through the air as children threw books, brooms, and anything they could get hold of at the chickens. The chickens screeched and flew about wildly trying to avoid the flying objects. Several of the girls who had been scratched on their hands and faces by the chicken's feet began to howl. Meanwhile, the secretary and the principals of the other schools, tried to remain dignified. But, as they tried to sit still, they wriggled their bodies about trying to protect themselves from being scratched. Ms Wen covered her face with her hands and turned to face the blackboard, not bearing to look at all the disorder and turmoil.

After the chickens had at last been chased away, the children couldn't calm down from their excitement.

The bell rang.

Highly embarrassed, Sang Qiao led the secretary and visiting principals away from the classrooms. On their way to the office, they heard Mrs. Qin calling to her chickens, ducks and geese. She looked as if she were walking in a deserted field after the crops had been harvested. She called frantically to the chickens, ducks and geese, pounding her feet on the ground. Many children followed her and also started calling to the chickens, ducks and geese.

Jiang Yilun went after her and called out, "What are you doing? What are you shouting for?"

Mrs. Qin rubbed her eyes and look at him, "Can't you hear me? I want to find my chickens, my ducks, and my geese!"

Sang Qiao invited the town secretary of culture and education into the office and looked stony faced as they had tea. Then, after the other principals arrived in the office and told funny stories about the class, the secretary asked Sang Qiao, "Mr. Sang, is your Yau Ma Tei Primary School a school or a farm?"

Sang Qiao sighed, and realised that the time had come for him to properly solve the problem. He told the secretary about the situation and about his ideas.

The other principals left, but the secretary stayed behind. He had been Sang Qiao's friend for many years, and Yau Ma Tei Primary School was his favourite school. He was determined to help Sang Qiao. That evening, Sang Qiao's school invited the local leadership to dinner. After dinner they went to the office to sit down together and discuss this problem. They talked late into the night and were all in agreement: Yau Ma Tei Primary School must solely be a school and have all the land to itself. That night, specific measures were implemented.

Four

Within three days, a house was being built for Mrs. Qin on the bank of a different part of the river.

They are still trying to get rid of me, thought Mrs. Qin as she stood leaning on her cane among her wormwoods. She thought of Qin Da, of their dream, of the wheat, of them walking around the field in the moonlight, of her exhaustion from the battle for her land with the district county ... And she cried in the wind.

The house was now built.

People came to ask Mrs. Qin to move.

She said, "If I wanted to move, I would have moved by now. A few years ago, you also built a house for me. Did I move?"

"This time, you must move."

"This is my home!"

They knew they couldn't reason with her and had to take desperate measures. Some strong men found a plank of wood that had once been part of an old door. One of the men picked her up and placed her onto the wooden plank. "Carry her away!" And they carried her away. Maybe she felt too old and tired to struggle, because she lay down obediently on the wooden board and didn't make a sound. When she was placed at the door of the new house, she would not get off the board.

Yau Ma Tei Primary School had sent a group of teachers and students to place things in the little house and to prepare a new space for the chickens, ducks and geese, which by now had been caught by the children.

By noon her new home was completely ready, and Mrs. Qin seemed at last to have accepted her fate. Everyone kept watch until dark to make sure she didn't return to the school. Sang Qiao breathed a long sigh of relief.

After dinner, as Sangsang was doing his homework, he was unable to concentrate. He saw a picture in his mind of Mrs. Qin lying down among the wormwoods. He put down his books and went to the field. In the distance he couldn't see the little house, only the wormwoods. The wormwoods stood silent in the moonlight, and he walked on as if a voice was calling him to them. The smell of wormwood grew stronger.

Sangsang arrived at the wormwoods and immediately saw that there was someone lying in the middle of them. He didn't feel afraid, or surprised, as he walked forwards and called, "Grandma!"

He heard Mrs. Qin's voice say, "Sangsang?"

Sangsang squatted down beside her. The wormwoods covered him.

"Grandma, you can't sleep here!"

"I won't go, I won't!" She kept repeating this like a child.

Sangsang stood up and looked around. Nobody else was around. He wanted someone to come and see that Mrs. Qin was lying in the wormwoods. But nobody came, and Sangsang silently sat down again beside her.

She said, "It's very late. You should go home."

Sangsang ran out of the wormwoods to the office and shouted to the teachers, "Mrs. Qin is lying in the wormwoods!"

Then he hurried to his home and announced loudly to his father, "Mrs. Qin is lying in the wormwoods!"

Sang Qiao and the teachers went to see what was going on, and in the beams of their flashlights saw Mrs. Qin curled up and lying silently among the wormwoods.

Sang Qiao told her to go back to her new house. She didn't lose her temper, but announced stubbornly, "I am staying here."

Sang Qiao called in the locals to help and instructed some of the stronger men to carry Mrs. Qin back to her new house on the same wooden board they had used earlier. She didn't put up a struggle and let them carry her away.

Sangsang slept badly that night. In his sleep he saw Mrs. Qin lying in the middle of the wormwoods. Early the next morning, he jumped out of bed, quietly opened the door, and ran to the wormwoods. He found Mrs. Qin lying there covered with frost. Sangsang sat beside her until the sun came up.

For the next week, Mrs. Qin's days followed the same cycle of first being found in the wormwoods and then being carried back home.

Everyone soon became tired of it and grew more and more impatient, "Damn it! Let her freeze to death!" And after moving her back home a few more time, everyone began to ignore her.

Two days later, she was found gathering up sticks and matting with which she began to build a hut in the place where her original little house had been. But before she could finish, it was torn down. She didn't give up, but went about gathering more sticks and matting and started building again. As before, before she could finish, it was torn down.

Some of the old people in the village declared to those wanting to keep on tearing down the hut, "She's trying to kill herself. Leave her alone."

Winter was coming.

Sang Qiao went to the wormwoods and saw a now very weak Mrs. Qin having great difficulty trying to support a broken mat with a thin bamboo pole.

He returned to his office and spoke to the local authorities who had come to inspect progress, "Let's talk about it again after the winter."

The next day, Sang Qiao instructed the community to build a temporary shelter in the northwest corner for Mrs. Qin to protect her through the winter.

Later, Sang Qiao stood at the southernmost point of Yau Ma Tei Primary School looking over to the wormwoods, and said to himself, *This old woman is hateful!*

Five

The remainder of the winter passed by peacefully.

Spring was approaching, and the children shed their

winter clothes and ran around in the sunshine. They felt a great sense of freedom now that the hard shell of winter was gone. Throughout the cold months they had worn thick cotton padded jackets and stayed in their houses with no desire to go outside and play. Their teachers observed that they dreaded leaving home to come to school, and dreaded leaving school to go home again in the severe icy winds. Winters on the plains were unforgettably cold. Their teachers all agreed that because the children didn't want to run around so much in the freezing winter weather, that they were much easier to supervise.

With the onset of spring, the children of Yau Ma Tei Primary School didn't want to go back to school. Looking up at the sun in the sky made them want to be outside all day and play in the fields, the lanes, and the rivers. When the bell rang they reluctantly entered their classrooms, but for the full forty-five-minute lessons, all they could think about was having more fun outside. The number of students who were sent to the office to be disciplined suddenly skyrocketed! And the campus that had been peaceful throughout the entire winter was suddenly filled with lively enthusiastic sounds, like the squeals and squawks of happy newborn baby animals.

One morning, a little second grade girl named Qiaoqiao was playing happily in the bamboo forest and completely forgot to go to school. She took a thin tree branch and banged on the bamboo poles as she walked around the forest. As she hit them gently, the bamboo poles, of different heights and sizes, made nice sounds that she sang along to. After enjoying this for a while, she went down to the river. The frozen water had now melted under the sun. The river flowed quite fast, and some yellow finches chirped musically as they perched on the gently blowing reeds. Qiaoqiao noticed a flower on the surface of the water, that was flowing from west to east. It shimmered in the ripples, and she couldn't take her eyes off it. It was a bright red rose!

Qiaoqiao kept her eyes on it as she climbed down the river bank. As she watched, the rose was about to drift right in front of her. She flung herself recklessly to the river's edge, held on to the reeds on the bank with one hand and reached down to the water with a branch in her other hand. She was determined to stop the flower. The river bank was wet and soggy from the melted snow and ice, and the reeds in Qiaoqiao's hands suddenly uprooted. Before she knew it, she had fallen into the water. A last glimpse of the flower flashed before her eyes and drifted away.

She choked on some water and struggled to get out of the river. Glancing up, she saw Mrs. Qin on the embankment with her back towards her, looking in the opposite direction.

"Grandma!" she cried.

Then the swirling water dragged her under. As she was about to sink and drown, she saw a figure flying towards her from above, like a black cotton jacket blowing in the wind.

Mrs. Qin had been watching her chickens foraging in the grass when she heard the girl's cry. Turning around, she had seen a child's face bobbing up and down in the water, her arms and hands reaching upwards. On hearing the desperate cry for "Grandma," she jumped down the embankment and dove into the river.

Dazed, Qiaoqiao felt hands grabbing at her trousers. They were not strong hands, because it took a long time before they successfully pushed her up and out of the water. As soon as she was safely on the bank, the hands let go. The water rang in Qiaoqiao's ears and the sun shone on her face. She felt as if she had awakened from a nightmare. She spat out some water, sat up, looked at the river, and cried.

Then Sang Qiao approached and asked her, "Why are you crying?"

Qiaoqiao pointed to the water, "Grandma ..."

"Who?"

"Mrs. Qin."

"What about her?"

"She is in the water ..."

Shocked, Sang Qiao yelled loudly for others to come, screaming, "Help! Help! Come quickly! Help!"

Then, he plunged into the river.

When she was pulled from the water, Mrs. Qin was out of breath. Lying in Sang Qiao's arms, many others arrived and surrounded them, witnessing the scene. Mrs. Qin was soaking wet, her silver hair dripped with water and her legs hung limp, swinging like pendulums. Her cheek was gashed and bloody, no doubt having been cut by a branch as she had thrown herself into the water. Her eyes were closed, and she looked as if she might never wake up.

The riverbank was in uproar, with cries of, "Call the doctor!" "Someone is dead." "Bring an ox." Asi and his ox are coming." "The ox is coming." "Please make way, please make way!"

Si arrived with his ox, wildly lashing it with branches in his efforts to make it go faster.

"Put her on the ox, quickly!"

"Give the ox some space！"

"Get out of the way！"

At last, the crowd retreated, making space for the ox and Mrs. Qin.

Mrs. Qin was laid across the back of the ox. The ten o'clock sun shone warmly down. Si led his ox as Mrs. Qin slept, making no movement.

An old man cried, "Make the ox go faster！"

The ox slowly picked up speed.

The little girl Qiaoqiao, in a state of shock, sobbed, "I fell in the river, and when I got out of the water I saw Grandma. I called to her ..."

Mrs. Qin still did not wake up. Everyone looked sad and disappointed. Sangsang stared at her, silent and bewildered.

Qiaoqiao stamped her foot and shouted, "Grandma！ Grandma！" Her cries tore through the spring air.

Sang Qiao, who had been directing the rescue, squatted wearily on the ground. His clothes were drenched in water from when he had rescued Mrs. Qin, and he shivered in the cold wind.

Qiaoqiao's father wiped away his tears and pushed Qiaoqiao forward, saying, "Call to Grandma, as loudly as you can！"

Qiaoqiao yelled as hard as she could.

Sang Qiao called Jiang Yilun and Wen Youju to him, and said, "Tell all the children to call out her name together. Maybe they can wake her up."

So all the children shouted loudly, "Grandma！" The sound was overwhelming.

Si, leading his ox, suddenly noticed a stream of yellow water flowing down the side of the animal. He took a closer look and saw that it was coming from Mrs. Qin's mouth. He pressed his ear to her back and smiled. Wiping the sweat from his brow, he drove the ox faster as Mrs. Qin's body moved rhythmically on its back.

Half an hour later, the ox let out a heavy sigh as Mrs. Qin was taken off of him and carried into her little house.

A woman shouted, "All men out!"

Sangsang's mother and several other women stayed in the house and changed Mrs. Qin's wet clothes.

The hut was a hive of activity with people coming and going until dark.

Six

Two weeks later, Mrs. Qin could at last get out of bed. Sangsang's mother made her three meals a day, and the female teachers of Yau Ma Tei Primary School and women from the village took turns in caring for her.

One day she said she wanted to go outside.

Sangsang's mother said, "Okay," and helped her to walk out of the house.

The sun shone brightly. It dazzled her eyes and she covered them with trembling hands. She felt that she had never before seen the sky so vast and blue. Although it was warm, because she was still weak and she felt a little cold.

Sangsang's mother advised her to go back inside, but she shook her head and said, "I want to go for a walk." As she helped her along, Sangsang's mother thought how thin and frail Mrs. Qin looked.

She walked to the campus. The children poked their heads out of the doors and windows and called, "Grandma!" over and over again. When she passed by the office door, the teachers all got up from their chairs and said hello to her. She nodded to them.

Sang Qiao brought a cane chair to her, "Sit down and rest."

She shook her head, "No, thank you. I want to walk."

Two weeks later, when she could walk by herself with no help, the people of Yau Ma Tei noticed that each morning Mrs. Qin, supported by her cane, walked to the market with a chicken or a duck or a goose. At noon, she came back empty-handed. After a while, the school children no longer heard the sounds of chickens, ducks, or geese.

Several times the teachers found that ducks from someone else's farm had got into the school garden, but Mrs. Qin drove them back to their own yard with a stick. Then, she stayed on guard by the garden in case they returned.

More and more children liked to go to the wormwoods, especially some of the girls who loved to visit Mrs. Qin in her little hut. Mrs. Qin braided their hair, and in the autumn, they asked her to paint their nails red. Mrs. Qin picked some impatiens, put them in a clay pot, added alum, and crushed and mixed them together. After painting their nails with the mixture, she covered them with flax leaves and bound them with lengths of straw. Four or five days later, when the leaves were removed, the girls had beautiful bright red nails.

Showing them off to those girls who hadn't had their nails painted, they boasted, "Grandma did it."

If a teacher found that a girl was absent from class, he would ask one of her classmates, "Go and look for her in Mrs. Qin's little house! "

Mrs. Qin loved to walk around on campus. That summer, her hearing had greatly deteriorated so that now everyone had to speak to her in loud voices so that she could hear what they were saying. Strolling around campus, she saw children laughing and she laughed with them even though she didn't know what they were laughing about! When children played sports on the playground, she sat with her cane on a bench and watched the game from beginning to end, as if she were watching a play. She had no idea what was going on! If, during a basketball game, the ball came towards her, she would try to stop it with her cane. However, now she was old, her reactions were slow and she often didn't succeed. The ball would roll past her and she and the children would laugh together. Sometimes, the ball rolled into the pond. A child would come up to her and ask, "Grandma, can I use your cane? " Even though she couldn't really hear, she could tell what he wanted and would hand over her cane.

One of her favourite things to do was to lean against the windowsill and watch an entire lesson take place from beginning to end. She couldn't hear a word, and even if she could have, she probably wouldn't have understood any of it. Occasionally, the students played a practical joke on her. Before their teacher arrived, they led Mrs. Qin up onto the teacher's podium. As she stood there, the children laughed. When the teacher came in and saw her standing in his place, he laughed too. Seeing them all laugh made her realise that the children were poking fun at her. She waved her cane about and pretended to hit them, before playfully leaving the classroom.

Often, when the teachers woke up in the middle of the night to the sounds of wind and rain, they would remember that they hadn't closed their classroom windows and doors. When they got up to shut them, they would see Mrs. Qin out in the dismal weather reaching up with her cane trying to close a window that she could barely reach.

She walked around the campus and looked after Yau Ma Tei Primary School for Sang Qiao.

When someone stole pods from the school, she would say to them, "Those pods belongs to the school!"

Those who remembered the Mrs. Qin of the past, now thought she was very amusing. When some old women saw her guarding the school's lotus pond so that nobody could pick the lotus seeds, they would think, *That crazy old woman!*

Incredibly, everyone in the school, from Sang Qiao, to the teachers, and to the children, now regarded Mrs. Qin as one of their own.

And so, the days went by.

One spring, Yau Ma Tei Primary School was recognised by the county education bureau for its continuous excellence in teaching and its outstanding landscaping of the grounds. The day came when the bureau invited a large group of visitors to a meeting in the school. For a long time, Sang Qiao had felt immensely proud of his accomplishments. Walking proudly around in the evenings, when he came to the edge of the lotus pond, the small bridge, or the woods, he couldn't help but sing to the heavens with joy.

The day before the meeting, he thought carefully about what must be done. Everything had to be perfect and flawless.

He strolled around the campus from corner to corner, checking on every last detail. When he saw that every little thing was spotlessly clean, Sang Qiao at last was satisfied. He sat in the large cane chair in the corridor outside the office with his legs crossed, and began to doze. Almost asleep, he heard some children chuckling. He opened his eyes and saw they were coming towards him.

"What are you laughing at?" he asked.

They told him that when they were having a lesson, Mrs. Qin had stood at the door listening. Then, she had gone to the back of the classroom and stood there until the class was over.

Sang Qiao smiled at this, but soon stopped laughing as he thought about how Mrs. Qin walked around the campus with her cane. He began to worry: *What should I do tomorrow if she decides to come into the classroom?* Over the past year, Mrs. Qin had begun to age very quickly and was now almost childlike.

That evening, Sang Qiao went to Ms Wen and said, "Please take Mrs. Qin into town to see a play tomorrow."

Ms Wen guessed the reason for Sang Qiao's request, and agreed.

The following day, before the visitors arrived at the school, Mrs. Qin happily left with Wen to see the play. However, Ms Wen didn't like sad drama, and so when they arrived at the theatre and she had settled Mrs. Qin into her seat, she left for the cultural station to meet with her friends.

The play began, but as she watched, Mrs. Qin realized she had seen it many times before. As she sat there, she suddenly remembered that she had promised to braid Qiaoqiao's hair, so she left the theatre and rushed back to the school.

When Mrs. Qin arrived back on campus, the school visitors were still there. As old and muddle headed as she now was, she knew deep down what she must do. So, instead of approaching the group, she took a detour and went back to her little house. She didn't leave it again until the visitors had left.

That evening, when Sangsang took Mrs. Qin a jacket that his mother had made for her, he saw that she was packing her things.

"Grandma, what are you doing?"

Sitting on the edge of her bed, throwing things into a big willow basket, she said, "It's time for me to move."

"Who has asked you to move?" I've heard from my father that in a few days he's going to knock down this little house and rebuild it for you. The grass and bricks have already been prepared."

She gently patted Sangsang's head, saying, "No one has asked me to move. I feel it is time for me to move."

Sangsang hurried home to tell his father.

Immediately, Sang Qiao and several teachers ran to her hut to stop her from packing and to persuade her to stay.

However, she wouldn't change her mind, but said calmly, "It's time for me to move."

In days gone by, no one could get rid of her; now, no one could get her to stay!

At first, Sang Qiao told his teachers, "Don't help her move her things." But, when he saw Mrs. Qin trying to lift her possessions one by one like an army of ants from morning till night, he changed his mind and asked the teachers and students to help her.

When Mrs. Qin had finally left Yau Ma Tei Primary School, all the students and teachers felt as if there was something missing. The children would still look out of their classroom windows during lessons.

Sangsang went to Mrs. Qin's new house every day.

After a few days, the other children also began to visit Mrs. Qin's new home.

Now that Mrs. Qin had left Yau Ma Tei Primary School, she felt a terrible kind of loneliness. She often stood behind her house looking for long periods of time towards the school. Although her eyesight was very poor and she could hardly see, she could imagine what the children were doing.

Spring and summer passed, and along came autumn.

On a rainy day, Sangsang stood under a tree near the school gate and looked over at Mrs. Qin's cottage. He noticed that there was no smoke blowing from the chimney and turned and ran home to tell his mother and father.

His father said, "Perhaps she is ill." And they all ran through the rain to the cottage to check on Mrs. Qin.

As expected, they discovered that Mrs. Qin was unwell.

The school teachers all took turns to watch over her for a week, but she failed to get any better.

"Let's take this opportunity to bring her back to live on campus, "said Sang Qiao. And he instructed workers to build her a house.

One fine day, Mrs. Qin was taken back to Yau Ma Tei Primary School and moved into the new house that had been built for her.

Seven

It was a typical day when Sangsang finished fifth grade and the summer vacation began. But by dusk, the sound of Sangsang's distressing cries made it clear to everyone that Mrs. Qin was dead.

She didn't die of illness or old age, but fell into the river again and drowned.

The last time she had plunged into the river was to save a child. This time is was simply to save a pumpkin for the school.

A few days earlier, she had seen a pumpkin hanging from a vine, almost touching the water. It had rained all the previous night, and that morning she saw that it was very nearly in the water. Seeing that the pumpkin was about to drop, she slid down the river bank and tried to pull it with a stick up and away from the water. She slipped on the muddy bank and tumbled into the river. Perhaps it was because she was now so old that she couldn't put up a struggle and slowly sank beneath the water. A woman washing clothes on the other bank saw Mrs. Qin trying to save the pumpkin, and called out to her to stop. Unfortunately, Mrs. Qin was too deaf and didn't hear her. Before the woman could do anything to help, Mrs. Qin had disappeared into the undertow. This time she didn't come back to life.

That night, all the teachers kept vigil over Mrs. Qin's body.

She was dressed in clothes that Sangsang's mother had sewn for her and laid out on a bed that had been especially made. A candle was lit at her head, and another at her feet.

Sangsang sat beside her. In the candlelight he thought Mrs. Qin looked very serene. As the adults came and went,

Sangsang didn't leave her side. Sometimes he sat there alone, but he was never afraid.

Sang Qiao cut a bundle of wormwoods with a sickle and placed them in the coffin with Mrs. Qin.

Many people came to see her.

According to local traditions, before sealing the coffin, a lock of hair from the deceased's children and grandchildren should be cut and placed beside the body. However, Mrs. Qin had no descendants.

Someone thought of Sangsang and asked his mother, "Will you cut a lock of Sansang's hair?"

She replied, "When Mrs. Qin was alive, Sangsang was one of her favourite children. She should be given a lock of his hair."

Someone brought a pair of scissors and called, "Sangsang, come here!"

Sangsang went over and bowed his head in readiness.

A lock of hair was cut off and wrapped in some paper. It would be with Mrs. Qin forever.

Mrs. Qin's funeral procession was grander than any that had ever been witnessed before in the history of Yau Ma Tei, and probably would never be rivalled in the future. The townspeople, teachers and children of Yau Ma Tei Primary School walked for more than a mile through the fields.

Sang Qiao chose the burial site. It was on a good piece of land. He said, "She always loved this land."

In front of the tomb was a large field of wormwoods that had been moved there from the school fields. The children came to water them every day to make sure none of them died. Today, they stand upright, their leaves fluttering in

117

the wind that blows from the fields, always giving off their unique fragrance.

(Selected chapters from *The Straw House*)

The Red Tiles

I finished my primary school in the house of straw, middle school in the house with red tiles, and high school in the house with black tiles. I was in the house with red tiles when the story took place. Even today, those red tiles flip through my memory like the pages of a book.

A circus arrived in Yau Ma Tei during a season when the reed catkins were in full bloom. Students bubbled with excitement all day.

Small town life is varied and colorful, but also lonely. A movie or a theatrical performance is enough to make everyone from the youngest to the oldest long for events like this with great excitement. As night fell, people would come from all over and gather in an empty field that had just been harvested. On a moonless night, you would see the roads glowing with lantern lights and flashlights among the walkers as they called out greetings to friends and families. The field would already be packed with people, while the lights of the latecomers on the approaching roads and paths flashed from every direction. If the movie or performance had already begun, those latecomers would run like refugees fleeing from war, their shoes pitter-pattering along the ground as they dashed hurriedly along.

Performances were rare however, taking place only five or six times a year. So that when such opportunities came along,

119

everyone in town would go crazy with excitement as if there were no tomorrow! During these times, the field would be noisy, with people pushing and shoving each other so that the crowd under the dark night sky looked like a black wave rushing from one side to another. If the field was next to water, a lot of people would be pushed into it, and we would hear their howls of frustration. Occasionally kids, who can be smarter than adults, would climb high up into the trees around the field. Sometimes there were about a dozen of them in one tree, sitting among the branches like big birds.

In my memories, I went to see countless movies when I couldn't find a good place to stand and watch. So, after a bit I would move and go behind the screen. I remember not being too disappointed however, because there was a big ditch behind the screen, and for me it was just as much fun to see what was going on back there!

Young boys of my age value this kind of opportunity more than anything. They are free to go crazy, climb trees, chase each other, fight with friends, be daring, and get excited about movie heroes. Therefore, we were always inquiring when the next entertainment would be coming to town.

Eight out of ten times, the events were held in our Yau Ma Tei Middle School playground. However, it was only once in a blue moon that a circus came along.

Our school had been busy for the entire three days before the arrival of the circus. We set up the stage, cleaned up the rooms, and added more tables to the dining room as the circus performers were going to stay on our campus. We were so excited that none of us were interested in studying any more. As the Chinese idiom goes, everyone had "a heart like

120

a capering monkey and a mind like a galloping horse."

Sweat dripped from San's clothes everyday.

San was a prefect who had the nature of a servant, as well as a desire to be in charge of others. However, he didn't have the talent to supervise, lacking the coolness and arrogance of a true leader. For this reason, his style of leadership was not to direct others and just sit back and watch them work, but to work alongside them. He didn't want to stand by idly doing nothing himself. When working, he was always the first to fetch the tools and get down to work, and the last to stay till the very end, cleaning up the mess alone when finished. Everyone has a role to play in life, and for San, he was a servant to his bones, and this would never change.

The school entrusted our class with welcoming the circus. San worked very hard and carried out all the work impeccably. Our headmaster, Mr. Wang, who usually had a gloomy expression on his face, smiled silently after his inspection.

The circus arrived in the afternoon. It came from a very distant place in a big boat towed behind a ship. There were monkeys, bears, horses, sheep, dogs, cats and other animals. There were also one or two dozen animal trainers. The circus master was a tough looking man in his mid-30s or 40s, with a huge body, a red shiny face, and two bright eyes under sword-like eyebrows. He always had his horse with him as he ordered us where to take the iron cages. His horse was enormous and as shiny as black silk.

And yet, despite the grandeur of the circus master, our eyes could only fix on a girl. She was sixteen or seventeen years old, and next to her stood two white puppies. As we carried the iron cages, we all looked at her secretly, feeling ashamed of ourselves for being so curious. The girls who were not working huddled together and stared at her as if she were a person they could only see in their dreams: a fairy floating from the sky.

The girl stood shyly by the river. She had a slim figure with a slender neck and long arms. Her forehead was smooth, while her eyes, nose and mouth showed an inexplicable charm. What was most fascinating was her captivating poise and gentle demeanor.

Her skirt, made of white silk, was charming, too. It was the first time we had seen a skirt. None of the girls in the town had ever worn one. When the breeze blew, her white skirt rose like a lotus flower blossoming upside down. Sometimes it was strong enough to lift her skirt high. She would turn her face slightly away from the wind, stretch out all her fingers to push the skirt down, while keeping her legs closed tight and her knees slightly bent. The two puppies that she held on leashes were of a kind we had never ever seen before. Their whiteness was unforgettable. They were small with long curly fluffy fur that covered their paws, ears and eyes. They played around her feet. Sometimes she would say, "Down, puppies!"

"Qiu!" the circus master said to her, "Stay here and watch the students move our things. I'm going to the classroom to have a look."

That's how we learned her name.

We whispered, "Her name is Qiu."

Qiu watched us moving everything. Her two puppies were very playful and kept running around. Sometimes she had no choice but to follow after them for a few steps, but she never left the river.

San worked harder than ever before. He was particularly enjoying taking command today, while doing the heaviest jobs himself. He had strong wide shoulders that could bear several times the weight that any of us could carry.

He breathed loudly, with two big front teeth exposed as he wiped away sweat, and seemed to be thinking, *I am a good servant who not only has strength, but is also willing to use his strength.*

"Qiu is watching San," said Ma, who was always very lazy.

I looked at Qiu and saw that she was looking closely at San. At that moment, San was carrying a huge box away from the boat on the river, straining with every step like a wharf laborer. The box was a little too heavy for him. Qiu looked worried. She felt bad for San, but didn't know how to help him.

"I can carry a box like that too," Ma said jealously. However, he couldn't even carry a small box! All of a sudden, Lin jumped into the boat, making it rock. Ma wobbled, tried to keep his balance by holding a big box, but eventually fell into the water, taking the box with him.

Lin and I laughed out loud and shouted, "Oh—"

Ma swam to the boat and grabbed the side with his hands.

He looked at the box that was floating on the water and shouted, "Lin, reach for the box with a bamboo stick!"

Qiu approached with her puppies.

San came back and saw the floating box. He quickly jumped into the water, swam to the box and brought it ashore.

Ma quietly cursed San.

Without getting angry, San simply walked away carrying the box on his head.

The circus had so many belongings that even though we had been working all day, three quarters of them were still on the boat. Extremely exhausted, we sat in the shed in front of the dining hall, and left San to quietly carry the rest of the things by himself.

Qiu sat by the river with her puppies watching San work.

After a while, Lin, annoyed by what Ma had said to him earlier, began chasing him around the table and pillars.

After they were done chasing each other, Ma suddenly stopped and pointed at the river.

We turned around and saw Qiu walking towards San. She handed him a handkerchief and asked him to use it to wipe his sweat. San refused to take it, but Qiu held her hand up high in front of his face. San hesitated for a moment, grabbed the handkerchief, rubbed his face vigorously, and quickly returned it to her. She took back her handkerchief and, with a smile, watched him carry another box.

Lin went back to chasing Ma again.

After dinner, we waited for San to wash all the dishes before heading to town. Ma put his arm on San's shoulder, turned his head around, winked, and then asked San, "Did that handkerchief smell good?"

"Get lost!" San furiously shook away Ma's arm.

We surrounded San and forced him to give an answer.

"There was a nice scent," he said at last.

We all laughed and continued on to town.

Ma whispered to me, "What a guy! He took her handkerchief

so he could smell it, and says it smelled like perfume!"

Two

Qiu walked leisurely through the campus with her two puppies. She first went to the lotus pond, then on to the school by the house with red tiles, and continued on to the house with black tiles. As she walked past the door of our classroom, we couldn't help glancing at the door from time to time to look out for her. When she headed to town with her puppies, our eyes followed her as she walked into the distance. Qiu was so special. We had never seen anyone like her and never imagined there could be such an amazing girl in our world.

The image of her, an elegant girl in a white dress with two puppies, became an everlasting memory for all the students in our school. In the years ahead, this image would flash through our minds like fireflies in the summer. A few years later, whenever we met by chance and recalled those days, one of us would always ask, "Do you remember Qiu?" And, at such times, we would also mention San!

Excitement in the village built up as the time finally arrived for the circus performance to take place.

That night, the crowd was more disorderly than ever before. People appeared from everywhere, packing the playground of our school like a basin of overflowing water. If a person at the back of the crowd was short, he couldn't see the stage at all. But he wasn't put off by this! He and others like him picked a forceful and courageous advocate and tried to take control of the situation. Their champion stretched out his arms and yelled, "You men in front ..."

The crowd at the back roared, "Sit down！"

After a while it seemed to have some effect as the heads in front lowered like sinking water. Some of them sat down, some knelt, and others squatted.

Every so often someone would forgetfully raise his head and everyone screamed, "Whose thick skull is that? Get down！" If the man didn't obey, he was attacked with flying mud and shoes.

When those in the front sat down however, they occupied more space than when standing. As a result, the front of the crowd swelled like dried mushrooms in water and shifted towards the back. When those at the back couldn't bear the wave of bodies any more, they formed another wave and shoved back to the front. Those in the middle were under the greatest pressure, being crushed from all sides！

All they could do was cry out in desperation, "Help！"

The uproar continued, making it impossible for the circus to perform.

The circus master stood looking anxiously at the chaotic restless scene.

As Qiu wandered around at the front of the stage, her puppies barked at the crowd.

Many in the audience screamed in shock, "Dogs！Dogs！"

This made the chaos worse. When Qiu realized this, she immediately took her puppies and disappeared behind the stage.

When they couldn't bear the shoving any more, the people at the front began to frantically push backwards. Those behind them immediately resisted, thrusting forward in revenge, and the subsequent wave of bodies rolled over and over, driving them all the way to the front of the stage again. The stage was high and made of clay. It blocked the crowd like a seawall. But when the back wave came ferociously forwards again, the sheer force caused about forty or fifty people to land up on the stage. Immediately, they felt more comfortable and relieved as they found themselves able to breathe more easily now they were out of the massive crowd. However, many of them were embarrassed to find themselves up there fully exposed to the public. Some of them had never been on a stage before. They panicked and wanted to get off. But when they saw the chaotic hoards beneath them, they realized it was safer for them to stay where they were. Some of them felt a sense of pure relief as if having survived a disaster ... as if they had been drifting, hopelessly lost at sea, and had suddenly reached the safety of an island.

A woman on the stage was holding her child. From the expression on her face, her disheveled hair and sweaty shirt, we could tell she was struggling to protect her son. She was about to cry. She hurriedly laid the child down, and the first thing he did after leaving his mother's arms was to pee at the front of the stage! It was unclear whether he did this out of sheer naughtiness, out of frustration at being held and squeezed, or out of the pleasure he felt from being freed. Either way, he pushed his abdomen forward, bent his knees and held his breath as he released a big arc of pee under the bright lights. People below the stage dodged, causing another tidal wave of bodies to surge. Meanwhile, the child giggled happily.

Yu, head of our town's Cultural Station, and Chang, head of our village militia, began to take charge. Yu suffered from tuberculosis. He smoked frequently and stayed up late at night writing plays and rehearsing, which resulted in a complexion as pale as paper. He was also born with a big mouth which appeared even bigger now that he was ill and getting skinny. He opened his enormous mouth as if to swallow the entire crowd into his stomach. He cursed, and shouted and pounded his fists in the air, but to no avail.

Chang's head shone under the light. He had not always been bald, but he woke up one morning to find that he had suddenly lost all his hair! As if he were training his militia, he stood at the front of the stage and gave orders for everyone to calm down. Since he was very tall, he was also known as Qin Dama (which means he was strong and huge like a carthorse). He had a majestic manner and held a position of power, which was enough to make his enemies and all the villagers fear him. However, the crowd by now was so out of control that his cries were useless. Drowning in the immense chaos, and caught up in the invisible force of a mob mentality, they could no longer control their own actions or emotions. This seriously frustrated Chang's sense of authority and his long face grew red with anger. He looked like he wanted to run and grab a gun and shoot into the sky above, in an attempt to startle and control the crowd. Later, he commanded two militiamen to take two of the most rowdy villagers away and shut them into a dark room in our school.

Chang finally got rid of everyone from the stage. Meanwhile, Qiu had been standing backstage watching what was happening.

After a long while, the performance still couldn't begin. The circus master, Yu, and Chang felt hopeless and disappeared behind the stage to discuss what to do next. The audience grew impatient and began to throw the straw they sat on towards the stage. For a moment, the strands flew like locusts through the air.

Someone under the stage shouted angrily, "Hurry up with the performance! Come on!"

Meanwhile, someone threw some straw at Qiu, and all of a sudden there were countless more handfuls being hurled aimlessly at her. She stood back and covered her face with her arms. One of her puppies broke free from its collar, rushed madly to the front of the stage, and barked at the audience. She ran to the stage to rescue the pup from the rain-like straw. We saw a strand of straw fall on her pretty face and realized she was about to cry.

San jumped onto the stage and shouted into the crowd, "All the boys in my class come up to the stage now!"

As we struggled through the crowd and got to the stage, San said, "There's no other way. It's up to us."

We all felt a sense of both heroism and impending doom.

San said, "We must stand in front, hand in hand, to form a human barrier, and hold the crowd back so they can't get onto the stage. None of us must let go of our hands!"

We stood on the stage, feeling like warriors, showing a desire to work together.

We jumped off the stage, stood facing it hand in hand, and stepped back. At this point, we felt the huge power of the crowd behind us. We all clasped hands tightly, and like a human rope held everyone firmly back. Our action, at least for now, prevented further disruption. After a while, the crowd, no more than ten metres behind us, began to calm down a little. But it was absolutely impossible to silence everyone.

The circus, which had delayed its performance for more than an hour, no longer expected things to go very smoothly.

The circus master said, "Let's start!"

Reluctantly, the show began.

The turmoil, like the pains of childbirth, didn't stop, but kept coming in waves bit by bit. We were soon sweating. My left hand held San's right hand, and I could feel his moist palm. I looked sideways and saw that his hair was drenched with perspiration that was dripping down his chin.

"Loosen your hand a bit, " I said to San, who gripped my hand so tightly that I was in pain.

But San kept a firm grip on me. He was so strong and didn't realize the might of his own strength. I had no choice but to endure my discomfort. I secretly cursed San, just as Ma would do! Not long after, we became overwhelmed.

Ma was the first to loosen his grip and said to Lin who was holding his hand, "Your fingers are like crab claws!"

San yelled, "Hand in hand! Hand in hand!"

In turn, we loosened and then tightened our hands several times to relieve the pain. Just as we felt defeated, the circus master's performance somehow managed to distract and calm the crowd. He wore a top hat, with trousers tucked into long leather boots. He rode a large imposing horse with a jet black coat and eyes as bright as stars. His hoofs stamped over the stage making a heart-shaking thunderous noise. In our town we kept only cattle and one or two small donkeys. Nobody raised horses. As a result, few people had ever seen one before. Consequently, we really admired this horse and were captivated by him. The circus master himself was magnificent. His long legs were straight and powerful. He steered the horse with great grace and made it perform all sorts of surprising movements on the stage. One moment, the horse ran like the wind, then, suddenly digging his hoofs in stopped abruptly, broke into a leisurely canter, and danced gracefully to the beat of the music. His master always looked serious, and his deep dark eyes gleamed wildly under his top hat.

After the horse, the monkeys came on to perform and turmoil broke out yet again. Monkeys were not as tall as horses so that the people at the back couldn't see them. All they heard was the laughter of those in front. They wanted to know what was so funny and got angry and surged forward. By this time, the crowd had had time to rest and so had regained some of its earlier strength. It kept on surging forwards until soon its full weight was upon us.

"Hold on! Hold on!" San bawled as he shoved people back with his behind.

Ma cried, "I can't hold on! I can't hold on!"

We were squashed against the stage, so we tried our best to stop the angry mob by digging our feet firmly into the ground.

Wheezing from sore dry throats, and with our eyes soaked in sweat so that we could hardly open them, we didn't have any chance to enjoy the performance on the stage.

"Stop the show!" Yu shouted to the circus master.

Relieved, we all relaxed. Ma was the first to release his hands and climb onto the stage. The other students quickly followed. After holding the crowd back alone for a while, San also climbed onto the stage. Now there were so many people squished up there that we couldn't stand it, so we left and went backstage.

Backstage was next to the hallway of our classroom. Qiu stood under the pillar with her puppies and gave us a thankful smile.

"She hasn't performed yet!" Yao said.

We felt sorry, as we were eager to watch her perform.

We sat wearily on the porch. It was nice and quiet here. San sat beside me, the smell of his sweat choking me. He was so tired that he lay down on the ground.

"The performance isn't going to continue today," Yao said.

I felt really disappointed and let out an involuntarily sigh.

We all lay down in a disorderly heap.

Lin was the first to sit up and said, "You're lounging around like a bunch of pigs in a pigsty!"

All the signs were that, due to the chaos, today's performance was coming to an end.

Ma said, "We should go to our headmaster and ask him to agree to let us open our classroom door so that we can fetch stools and tables for the people at the back to stand on. Once they are able to see the show, they won't make any more noises."

San suddenly stood up and said, "I'll talk to him!"

I went with him.

Our headmaster, Mr. Wang, had predicted that the circus would not be able to perform any more that day. He had returned to his office. We found him sitting in a rattan chair drinking tea.

He listened to what San was saying and asked him coldly, "Will you take responsibility for any loss or damage to the tables and stools?"

San couldn't agree to this immediately, and so we returned to the porch.

"What a useless prefect you are!" Ma said.

"It's no use! No use!" said San.

"But of course we can take the responsibility!" Ma said. "When the performance is over, we'll stand in a row at the exit and keep an eye on everyone as they leave. No one will be able to steal any stools or tables."

San sat in silence.

The ground was noisy, and the sky was full of dust under the lights. Everyone was yelling, "Hurry up and perform!"

Ma shouted at San, "Do you dare open the door of our classroom?"

Lin mocked, "San won't dare! He isn't brave! He is a sissy!"

I retorted, "Don't you call San a sissy!"

In the crowd, some local ruffians were threatening to rush to the back of the stage.

Wanting to make trouble, they were shouting, "Let the bear go!"

Qiu looked at us in fear.

The circus master didn't realize how wild the angry locals could get, so he said to Yu, "Mr. Yu, we should start performing despite the disorder."

Ma whispered a few words to San and then dragged Lin and several of us towards the crowd.

San called to me to follow him to the house with red tiles. He took the key to our classroom from his trouser belt and opened the door. We walked into the classroom in the dark and then headed back to the crowd, each carrying a table on our heads.

San told us, "Ma has gone to get others to help us to carry the tables and stools. And he said he would ask the other class prefects to open all their classroom doors too."

"What if they don't agree?"

"Ma said he would tell them that our headmaster has given his permission."

"But he didn't give us his permission!" I said.

San fell silent. He felt helpless and didn't know how to handle Ma's boldness and the way he had of doing whatever he wanted. But he had no time to judge Ma, especially as no one else had dared to come up with any ideas. He felt confused, but followed anxiously along.

Ma was a daredevil and never considered the consequences of his actions. He always had to be doing something risky and exciting, as if his life depended on it. He was always lazy, late for class in the morning, and slept at his desk. However, he always gained loads of energy whenever he thought up ideas for interesting exploits! Sometimes he was even very smart. When others could see no good ending to one of his risky escapades, he would come up with an amazing idea that would somehow put an end to the crazy situation that had been brought about by his idea in the first place!

Ma spread the word, and all the class prefects opened their classroom doors. At once, all the people in the grounds flocked to the houses with red tiles and black tiles and carried away all the tables and stools, leaving the classrooms empty. It was like watching a stampede of ten thousand galloping horses and a group of bandits running down the hill to fight an army. A stair-like bleacher was erected. It prevented people farther away from the stage from creating a disturbance. By now it was getting late, order had been restored, and nobody wanted any more trouble.

Qiu's performance was charming. Her two puppies performed simply and without much skill, which only served to draw the audience's attention to Qiu herself. Strictly speaking, this was not a circus act. However, the crowd didn't mind. As they stared at Qiu, none of them cared that the puppies didn't make any amazing or exciting moves, because by now, Qiu herself had captivated and mesmerized these simple country people.

I crouched near the stage. The stage lights were bright and shone clearly on Qiu.

I glanced at San and saw that he was sweating.

The fact was that even though Qiu simply walked her dogs around the stage, it was enough to hold their attention and keep the audience silent.

After the show ended, we felt dazed, like a bird in the trees that had been startled awake from a peaceful sleep in the night sky. As the crowd began to depart, the scene before us made our spirits sink as we looked in despair at the horribly messy grounds.

It was about midnight. In the moonlight, the staggered tables and stools were strewn about like donkeys, horses, cats, and dogs that lay dead from the plague.

San was dumbfounded.

Ma was also stunned.

So much damage had been done, and it was difficult to move the tables and stools back into the classroom.

Headmaster Wang stood on the edge of the grounds and looked at the field. Without a word, he angrily stamped out his cigarette butt and left.

A group of students went back to the dorm and lay down.

When San asked them to give him a hand with putting the tables and stools back, they answered, "We didn't take them out!" He was desperate and began to beg for their help.

Ma approached the prefects one by one, half reminding and half threatening, "You lot were the ones who actually opened the doors of your own classrooms!"

The prefects didn't know what else they could do and so they called some of their classmates to the field. The tables and stools from each class were mixed together, and the first thing they needed to do was to distinguish which ones belonged to which classroom. A few flashlights beamed across the grounds, and from time to time we heard, "This is our table. This is our stool."

San felt bad and continued working nonstop.

Everything was such a mess that Ma also helped. Unused to heavy work, he looked very ungainly and clumsy as he went about his tasks!

I felt Lin poke me as he said, "Look!"

Qiu, with her two puppies roaming around her feet, was carrying a small stool as she followed behind San. She helped us for a long time, only stopping because the circus master repeatedly ordered her to go and rest.

After Qiu had gone, we carried on working to the point of exhaustion.

Ma said, "Let's go back to the dormitory for a break and continue later!"

Except for San, we all returned to the dormitory. We had a long rest and didn't wake up until Pockmark Bai rang the bell. Rubbing our bleary eyes, we rushed back to the grounds.

The sun was rising and San was still carrying the remainder of the tables and stools. His movements were slow, and he was obviously exhausted. When we reached him, his eyes were red and his face was covered with beaded sweat.

Qiu got up to help him move the remaining tables and stools.

Three

The circus didn't leave directly after the performance. Mayor Ming announced that he would return in two days, and that he had asked the circus to stay on and to perform again then.

So, the circus people and their animals continued to live on our campus. When not performing, they wandered around the school, strolled around town, or fished by the river. Between classes, students ran to the cages, plucking grass or grabbing candies to feed to the animals.

Qiu spent all her time outdoors. Alone, she walked her puppies and sat in the field or by the river. She came to our dorm twice, but refused to enter the room and stood outside the door. She wondered what detention San had received. San had been washing dishes for Ma, who in return had helped San write a three-page letter of apology to the school and pay for two damaged tables. After this, Headmaster Wang had forgiven him. When Qiu heard this, she was deeply relieved.

We were always happy to see Qiu.

San now seemed content to carry out his day-to-day

humdrum duties. Not only did he wash the dishes three times a day for Ma, but he also washed the dishes twice for me, and even once for Lin.

That evening, we went from the dormitory to the classroom for evening prep. We saw Qiu and San talking beneath a tree. Ma pointed at them. We uttered, "Ao!" and ran into the classroom.

We didn't want to study, and several of us sat together chatting and gossiping.

Ma made sarcastic remarks about our math teacher, saying, "Mr. Jiang may be fierce, but he's such a slowpoke! One day, the cotton jacket he was wearing caught on fire. Instead of putting out the fire, he slowly looked at his jacket and asked, "Hmm, I wonder where this fire came from?""

Yao, who had two front teeth missing and covered his mouth like a shy girl when he spoke, said, "When I was in elementary school, my Chinese teacher, nicknamed Yang dumb dumb, was a fool who shared a house with his brother. They didn't get along well, and so one day he climbed up onto the house with a saw and cut in half seven of the wooden beams. He said that half of the house belonged to him because it was a house left to them by his father!"

Lin was in the middle of ridiculing our headmaster when all of a sudden San burst into the classroom.

"Quickly! Come with me! The circus master is harassing Qiu!"

"Where?" I asked.

"By the lotus pond."

"How do you know this?" we asked San as we followed.

"She told me to follow her."

We ran blindly and had no idea what we would do. We ran past the porches of the houses with red tiles and black tiles, hearing the students inside asking, "What's going on out there?"

That night was moonless and windy.

We followed San to a place not far from the lotus pond and slowed down. As we approached the pond, we all trod lightly, making no sound, like cats trying to steal dried fish. We planned to suddenly jump out in front of the circus master who was bullying Qui and take him completely by surprise.

The lotus leaves in the pool rustled in the night wind.

The two puppies whined.

"Don't move!" ordered Ma harshly.

Yao shone his flashlight.

In the light, we saw the tall figure of the circus master running away, like a galloping horse.

Qiu cried as the autumn wind blew. You couldn't hear her crying unless you listened carefully. There was no anguish, no resentment, no despair in her crying. It was just a very little sad sound.

The two puppies clung to her, whimpering.

Qiu sat staring at the edge of the pond, as if she had lost something and was thinking about how to get it back.

We were tired and sat down on the grass.

Qiu gradually stopped crying.

A faint moon appeared in the sky.

We saw Qiu hugging her puppies as she fell asleep on the grass by the lotus pond.

We didn't go back to our dorm room, but, bewildered, stayed with her until dawn.

When the sun rose, she looked at us, her head resting on her knees and a few tears in her eyes.

We went back to the dormitory.

At noon, Lin stood in front of the dormitory and exclaimed, "There's that guy ... riding his horse!"

We all ran to the door to have a look.

We saw the circus master on his horse, racing frantically around the field. He was leaning forward, with his hair flowing behind him, and his clothes billowing like a sail in the wind. After dashing around madly for a while, he allowed the horse to slow down and walk through the field and down to the river. He seemed calm now, and his face looked healthier in the midday sun. We subconsciously admired him as he bent down over his horse, reached to the ground, and pulled up some hay to put it into its mouth.

Meanwhile, the mayor had returned, and the circus would perform that night.

That afternoon, Ma took a handful of croton seeds out of his pocket and gave them to San, who scattered them into the horse feed.

The handful of seeds brought huge disgrace upon the circus master during the evening performance.

He rode his horse onto the stage and saw Mayor Ming sitting in the front row. He took off his hat and bowed slightly in acknowledgement. At that very moment, the horse, with a loud neigh, gushed out a load of shit!

The audience roared with laughter.

The handsome horse now looked ugly and disgusting because of all the poop! Its buttocks were sticky and there was shit running down its legs. It made the stage filthy as it trod in its own mess, splattering it all around.

The audience laughed nonstop!

The circus master turned red with anger.

The horse droppings flowed steadily and the stench got so bad that the audience in front ran to the back.

At last, the circus master dismounted, led his horse away, and retreated awkwardly backstage.

Four

At dusk on the day of the circus' departure, Qiu came to our dorm, her hair straggly and strewn. This time she entered before we even let her in. She looked haggard with traces of shame and shock in her eyes. Her shoulders trembled ceaselessly, and she had a look of desperation in her eyes that cried out for help.

It reminded me of the dove I had caressed earlier. That afternoon, as I was picking willow flowers, I suddenly heard a sound coming from above me. Looking up into the clear blue sky, I saw an eagle chasing a dove. As I watched, it was very obvious that one was strong and the other was weak. It seemed that the eagle was made of iron with wings like two sharp knives, while the dove was merely like a sheet of thin tissue paper. The dove flapped hopelessly in the air. When the eagle struck, it fluttered down to land in front of me. The look in the dove's eyes was exactly the same as in Qiu's eyes.

I stood quietly at the door, along with Ma and several of the others. We all felt very protective of Qiu.

"I'll never travel with the circus again." She clasped her hands around the frame of a bunk bed and cried.

Ma said, "The circus will come looking for you."

I said, "Hide in the bamboo forest in the back!"

They all agree with me. We let Qiu and her two puppies jump out of the back window and run into the bamboo forest.

From that very moment, the bamboo forest held a secret!

We followed Qiu and we all sat down in the depths of the forest. Ma said to Qiu, "Go home! Go back to your parents."

Qiu told us that she had no idea who her father was. Her mother had been in the circus, too. However, one day while performing in a strange town, her mother had met a man and gone away with him, leaving Qiu, only three years old, all alone.

At prep that evening, some of us were missing because we had gone with Qiu to the bamboo forest: me, Ma, San, and Yao.

When the moon came out, we saw fog floating across the forest. As the wind rose, shadows of bamboo flickered over our faces. We were inexperienced and had no idea about how to solve this kind of problem. We were as confused here in the bamboo forest as we had been the night we had spent by the lotus pond.

Before dawn, we heard the sound of horseshoes. We crawled out of the bamboo forest to see the circus master riding his horse around the edge of the field, like a hunter stalking its prey. We told Qiu to stay in the bamboo forest and not to come out for anything. When we were back in class, we looked out of the window and saw the circus master tie his horse to a tree near the playground and begin to walk around the campus.

That evening, Ma, San and I hired a boat from our town so that we could take Qiu to the safety of Ma's home in the village of Wu, which was 15 miles away. Cautious and afraid, we handed her over to Ma's grandfather and made our way back to school.

The circus couldn't leave because nobody could find Qiu, which made the circus master very angry. He found our headmaster, Mr.Wang, and told him he thought that Qiu must had been hidden by his students. The headmaster was very angry and told the teachers in charge of every class to interrogate each of us in turn.

We were called to the office separately, but we all insisted, "I don't know! I'm not hiding anyone!"

When nobody at the school could find her, the circus master went to Mayor Ming, who asked all the villagers to look for her. The circus master insisted that there was a great possibility that she was being hidden somewhere in the school, and so Ming called Mr.Wang and demanded, "Your students are outrageous! Look again! You must find the girl!"

The circus master strode around anxiously all day long. His eyes were bloodshot and glowed with ferocity. Whenever he bumped into us he stared at us with an intense and skeptical look that made us terrified of being found out. At noon, he galloped his horse wildly around the playground, whipping it again and again to make it go faster and faster. All at once, the horse rushed out of the playground, carrying him like arrows flying through the sky, before plunging into the river. Thoroughly drenched, he clambered out while keeping a tight hold on his horse and continued his search in the reeds.

Two days later, the circus suddenly disappeared, before we had even got up. That morning, Ma's grandfather, who was in his seventies, walked onto the campus to find us.

He called us aside and said, "Yesterday evening, a man riding a black horse came to the village. At the time, Qiu was helping me pick persimmons. The man called for her to go with him."

Next, the old man held out to us five colored biloba (red, green, yellow, purple, blue) and said, "She asked me to give these ginkgo to your prefect."

We never saw Qiu again.

Qiu was just a flash in our life, like a rainbow after the rain that only stays in the sky for a moment and then disappears forever. But she left an indelible mark in our memories.

Later, we heard that the circus master knew Qiu had been hiding in Ma's home because it had been revealed to him by one of our classmates.

As for the colored biloba: our understanding was that Qiu meant to give them to five people: me, Ma, San, Lin and Yao. "To your prefect" had just been a vague statement. Nevertheless, as our prefect, San thought that all the biloba belonged to him and took them for himself.

About a year later, Lin was looking for a key in San's bed and accidentally came across a small bag under his pillow. He opened the little bag and inside were five colorful biloba.

Ma said, "Divide them up, and we will take one each."

We all took one and left the purple one for San.

When I was about to graduate from the house with black tiles, I heard a rumour that Qiu and the circus master had fallen in love, got married, and given birth to a girl as beautiful as Qiu.

144

The White–bearded Old Man

After getting out of bed, I walked out of the house and saw a boy standing in the yard. We stared at each other curiously.

He was exceptionally good looking, about seventeen or eighteen years old. His hair was as black as ink, naturally curly, and flopped untidily down over his eyebrows. His skin was smooth and soft; the complexion of a girl. If it weren't for the straight masculine nose and the line of dark fuzzy stubble above his upper lip, he could quite easily have been mistaken for a beautiful young woman.

"Elder brother Xuan, "he called with bowed head, shyly rubbing his hands together.

"Who are you？ "

My father poked his head out of the door and said, "He is Liang."

Liang？ Is this the boy who took off his clothes when he was a child and ran naked in the snow？

That winter, many years ago, I had taken a net into the field so I could catch some birds. It had been snowing for three days and had finally stopped. The ground was still covered in thick snow that was half a foot deep and sparkled brightly in the sun. I was setting up my net when I heard a group of children in the distance. "Oh, oh, " they cried cheerfully. I looked around and saw a little naked boy running across the snow.

That naked boy was Liang. He was only six years old at the

time.

He was an unusual boy. From the time he came into the world, his brain had always been filled with all kinds of imaginations and strange thoughts. It appeared that he was a little slow-witted and simple. So, on that day, it wasn't clear if maybe he had been tricked by the older children (who often fooled him because of his naivete), or perhaps it had been his own strange idea to take off all his clothes and run naked through the snow.

Liang rolled in the snow like a piece of sparkling pink meat.

"Liang!" I threw down my net, "Get dressed!"

He put his little hands on his chest and, tilting his head, looked at me and said, "Hei and the others said that I wouldn't dare to go naked!" Then, he ran off, his skin frozen and white, like glossy silk. He rushed around, his head bobbing up and down, his pink bare feet splashing through silver snowflakes.

The children jumped around in the snow and clapped their hands, "Oh! Oh!"

I wanted to stop him, but I was inexplicably caught up in the excitement with the others. I lost all reason that an adult should have, and I too joined in the fun and watched him running cheerfully in the snow.

He ran all over the vast snowfield. A huge band of children and I formed a large semicircle and followed him to the far side.

There was thunderous shouting with joy in the quiet wilderness.

A soft white blanket covered the entire field. Liang's delicate skin was frozen, bright red and glowing like a warm rosy light. As he ran, he left behind him small footprints, some shallow, some deep, that broke up the smooth snowy terrain.

All of a sudden, he fell down. He sprinkled snow all over his body until he looked like a fluffy duckling. Then, he rolled over and over gleefully until his face and head were also buried.

The children stood in a circle, looking like a group of little madmen, jumping about and shouting.

He stood up-a pure white child!

He shook himself-and became a pink child!

A strong wind blew violently, making the snow swoosh and swirl, and everything became blurred in the whiteness. Liang was hidden from view and disappeared. As the wind died down, they heard him cheering as he gradually came back into sight.

He was tired and so was standing very still.

We ran over and looked at him quietly.

The snow on his hair was melted with sweat, his hair was black and shiny and looked even darker against the white snow. His two small buttocks were extremely red. As he exhaled through his wet mouth, his breath was like a cloud of pale blue fog. Between his legs, his little penis was frozen and contracted, looking like a baby bird that had just hatched from its shell. His body seemed to glow in the cloud of pale blue fog of his cold breath. His eyes were full of curiosity and he was blinking happily. It looked as if he couldn't feel any coldness in the freezing cold and icy snow. His mother arrived and wrapped him in a big quilt. He wriggled happily inside it, and after a while poked out his little head and waved his tiny hands ...

Ten years had passed, and he had grown into such a handsome young man.

"You are Liang!" I recognized him and said quickly, "Come into the house and sit down."

He stood still, "I sent you letters. Did you receive them?"

"Letters? No! Where did you send them?"

"To the Beijing Chinese Department."

"You should have sent them to the Chinese Department of Peking University."

"Oh ..." Realizing he had written the wrong address, he nodded awkwardly.

"Come in."

He still refused, and took a stack of cigarette rolling papers from inside his jacket pocket.

"Brother Xuan, I know you are a writer now. The day before yesterday, I read your novel ..."

He hesitated and his speech faltered as he stared at me cautiously and said, "Brother Xuan ... I ... I want to be ... to be a writer, I have always dreamed of this. This ... This is a story I wrote, can you help me ... Will you take a look?" He handed the stack of cigarette papers to me.

I took it from him.

He looked unsure and embarrassed, rubbing his hands together and repeating, "I am not good enough ... in fact my writing is probably laughable to a writer like you!"

My father came over and whispered to me, "He is mentally ill. My heart skipped a beat, and when I looked into Liang's eyes I knew that there was something wrong: his eyes were dull and expressionless, and always fixed in one place.

"I am about to finish writing a novel of 300, 000 words called 'Breakdown' ..." He repeated this over and over again. He spoke in a low voice as if he was on autopilot and didn't really realize what he was saying.

I turned over a page of his story—

> ... Why do we get sick? Because we have a lot of machines, cold machines, high blood pressure machines, encephalitis machines, malaria machines, myocardial infarction machines ...
>
> Not long ago, my brother was actually oppressed by a cold machine.
>
> These machines are in the hands of a little granddaughter named Little Bee, her grandpa is the head of the National Security Department. Little Bee is very cute ...

I couldn't understand these bizarre words. I wanted to laugh, but knew I mustn't. I looked at Liang's handsome face and into his empty eyes, and said, "I will read your story very carefully."

Liang looked at me and began to tremble slightly, and then more and more noticeably. He opened his mouth and wanted to say something to me, but the idea seemed to be trapped inside him. He wanted to speak, but nothing came out. Finally, he bowed to me and left.

When he had gone, my father told me all about Liang.

Liang's illness was partly related to an incident in the village's ancestral hall.

The ancestral hall stands on the bank of the river at the front of the village. It is the tallest building. The villagers live in houses built with grasses and mud walls. The richer families have houses with walls built of both tiles and adobe, and all the roofs are made of grass. Only the ancestral hall has walls built with thousands of flat blue bricks. These types of bricks are no longer made by the old brick-making factory. The roof of the ancestral hall is covered with tens of thousands of pieces of semi-circular tiles. Inside, the girders are round, thick, and strong, and the rafters are made out of fine quality wood. The ancestral hall has stood on the shore of this river for many many years.

Every year, the ancestral hall was used to hold the annual festival that paid tribute to the esteemed ancestor, Qingming. It also had other uses, such as to imprison men and women who had eloped. After their capture, it was said that part of the punishment for both the men and the women was to strip off all their clothes and make them parade naked in front of the wooden tablets inscribed with the family names of their ancestors. Many people would come to watch and to shout insults at the offenders. The hall would also be used as the place where anyone who had disrespected their parents or elders would be punished. They were tied up, commanded to kneel down and to repent. Then, while in front of the ancestral tombstones, the elders would educate them on the correct ways to behave.

It is believed that more than one person died there throughout those years.

Later, the ancestral hall was requisitioned for use as a school office.

There were many creepy sayings linked to this ancestral hall. Teachers who had slept there told frightening tales about how they had been shackled at night. Things like they wanted to shout, but couldn't shout. They wanted to move, but couldn't move. Just before five o'clock in the morning, they would wake up feeling cold and sweaty, their clothes clinging to their bodies.

They would hear a strange noise on the roof that sounded as if someone was throwing stones. They would lie in bed waiting for the stones to roll down from the roof so they could go back to sleep. But the constant clatter of stones hitting the roof didn't stop, and they'd never heard the sounds of them hitting the ground.

One winter while finishing her dinner in the cafeteria, one of the female teachers remembered that she still had a lot of homework to mark. On her way to the office in the ancestral hall, she saw a short white-bearded old man standing at the door. He was dressed all in white. The teacher screamed and the lamp fell to the ground and shattered into pieces.

On hearing the noise, all the male teachers rushed out and asked, "What's the matter? What happened?"

The female teacher was stunned and very quiet. After a few moments she said, "White-bearded old man! Standing at the door, a white-bearded old man!"

The male teachers ran to the canteen looking for weapons, screaming, "The white-bearded old man!"

In a short while, the people of the village arrived holding countless flashlights that looked like searchlights at the frontier. However, even though the people turned the place upside down, the white-bearded old man was never found.

After that, the "white-bearded old man" became a topic that people in the village often talked about. A practical joker, walking along the road at night with his friends would scream, "The white-bearded old man is coming!" Everyone would scream and run away, and the sound of their pounding feet could be heard under the dark night sky. Then someone would fall down. "AHHH, "he would scream, before getting up in a panic and continuing to run. Someone else would fall into a muddy pond, emerging like a clay figurine. The clay man would desperately rush onward, splattering many of the others with mud along the way. Those who shouted and yelled the loudest were actually not the ones who were the most afraid. Although they felt a little scared, they also enjoyed the thrill of feeling their hearts skip beats with excitement.

The "white-bearded old man" was often used by adults to scare children: "You misbehave one more time, and I will give you to the white-bearded old man!" The children immediately quieted down and became very obedient.

My father was the principal of the school. My home was on the campus, very close to the ancestral hall. The chances of my being bothered and tortured by the "white-bearded old man" were more than that of others. One night, walking towards the ancestral hall with only a lamp, my father tried to convince people that the "white-bearded old man" might be the illusion of the light from his lamp shining through the branches of a sycamore tree in front of the house that reflected onto the white wall. No one believed him. I, of course, did not believe him either. Even if I saw the dark grey ancestral hall during the day, I would panic. After dark, I didn't dare walk past it, thinking that the white-bearded old man really did stand at the door of the hall. If

I went to see a movie and came back late at night, I would take a different route that required me to go around the pond so that I didn't need to go past the front door of the ancestral home. In an attempt to find courage, I would sing loudly the most spirited song "Climbing the Tiger Mountain," from the movie "Taking Tiger Mountain by Strategy."

The most rigorous punishment that teachers used in our school was to make students stand all alone in the ancestral hall with the door closed.

Of course, this severe disciplinary measure was only used once or twice a year as a last resort. And then, it had to be used during the day.

Liang's teacher was Mr. Huang. Because the teacher was the third of three brothers, everyone called him Mr. Three. Mr. Three taught in the old days at a private school, and he was so familiar with the San Zi Jing (the Three Character Classic) and Bai Jia Xing (the Hundred Family Names) that he could even recite them backwards. When teaching, he often revealed traces of the old ways. For example, he didn't like to read, but liked to sing and to nod his head. In addition, he still wore the old cotton baggy trousers from the old days. The crotch of his trousers was so big that it almost looked like he had a rabbit hiding in there. The students didn't respect him very much and often laughed about his trousers behind his back. But he was a proud and dignified man and asked the students to show respect.

Liang had been born with a simple mind and there were endless strange thoughts swirling around in his head. He often asked questions that Mr. Three didn't know the answers to. Since Mr. Three couldn't answer his questions, Liang was disappointed and often wrote his stories in secret without showing them to anyone. This greatly annoyed Mr. Three and he wanted to teach "this cranky guy" a lesson. One day, a student who liked to please his teachers, told him, "Liang wrote another story ... about the ancestral hall. I saw it. Liang also said that he would tear down the ancestral hall!"

So, Mr. Three sent Liang to the ancestral hall, "Did you write another story? Do you want to tear down this ancestral hall! How dare you! You just try!" Finished, he closed the door and walked angrily away. This was probably the first time in the history of the school that a student had been kept in the ancestral hall in the evening after school. Mr. Three left and went to dinner.

The night grew very dark.

My father came back from a town meeting and passed by the door of the ancestral hall. He heard an intermittent groan inside. He was shocked. He turned on his flashlight and saw Liang leaning far out of a window. His head was stuck and he couldn't seem to move. His hands were gripping the outside of the windowsill in desperation, as if there was something in the darkness behind, chasing him, and he was struggling to get away. My father rushed over, pushed Liang inside, slammed the window shut, and opened the door.

Liang did not speak, but he refused to leave the corridor.

"What did you see?" asked my father, noticing the cold sweat on his forehead.

He didn't say anything; he just cried.

My father finally persuaded him to go home.

The next day, when he returned to school, my father noticed something different about Liang compared to before. In particular, the way he looked at people ...

Had his family tried to get the school into trouble?

No; his family only noticed there was something mentally wrong with Liang a couple of weeks later. Some people suggested to his father that because he had a new house built without a Feng Shui Master to come and have a look, that it might be possible that his house was built on the wrong place. Later, his father invited a Feng Shui Master to their new home and he told him that it was built on the wrong place. His father immediately demolished the house. However, after doing that, Liang still wasn't cured, but was getting worse and worse. Therefore, he had to drop out of school. Liang was writing all the time, but no one knew what his writing was about. His family confiscated his papers because they were panicking that his mental illness was getting worse. So, he ended up collecting cigarette packages to write on instead. (In those times, cigarette packages had very beautiful illustrations on them and people would collect them for fun.)

That night, I lay in bed reading Liang's story. Despite the ridiculous words, countless misspellings, and lack of punctuation, I read like a beast that has been hungry for a long time and suddenly catches sight of his prey. Intently, I chewed over those strange and magical words. As I read, my breathing became rapid and shallow. This was an absurd world, like a broken piano, like music without harmony, like an unmusical person playing wrong notes ... a conflicting and discordant sound. But I was slammed by an invisible, unforgettable force, and from time to time my heart jolted like the last persimmon hanging in the wind. A while later, another wonderful emotion washed over me, and I felt the existence of a spiritual world outside of this material world. His story surprised me and I found I still had mysterious feelings that had not awakened within me.

I couldn't help but throw the story onto my bed and pace earnestly up and down my room.

This child's imagination was so bold that it made my soul tremble. His unique ideas and keen sense of emotion were simply unbelievable.

I was ashamed of myself and felt awkward and sad at my own lack of imagination. It should be him, not me, who had become a novelist. However, I was a man of sound mind after all, and he was but a simple-minded fool, a body without a soul. Therefore, all the words on the cigarette packages were no more than idiotic dreams and crazy ideas, not stories ... he may never be able to write novels.

I pushed the door open and went out into the cold night. I didn't go back into the house for a long time ...

The Spring Festival was over and there were only a few days left of my holiday before the school term started. It was time to go back to Beijing.

At dusk, it began to snow. Carrying a suitcase, I made my way to the boat dock. In the distance I saw Liang standing by the edge of the river. Standing there, he met my eyes and stared at me. It was no longer snowing heavily, but his hair and his shoulders were covered with two inches of snow. It was possible that he had been standing there for a long time.

"Liang!"

"Brother Xuan."

"Why are you standing there?"

"Waiting for you. You said that you would be leaving today."

I put my suitcase down onto the snow and looked at him. The snow on his eyebrows was frozen, his face was blue and purple with cold, and his body was shaking. I brushed the snow off his hair and shoulders for him. He didn't say anything, as if his soul were frozen.

"Go home, Liang."

From his pocket, he pulled out a thick book bound from all the cigarette packages covered with his writings, and handed it to me with both hands, "Brother Xuan, this is my novel 'Breakdown' that I wrote about the ancestral hall. Could you help me introduce the novel to the people in Beijing so that it can be published?"

Who will publish this kind of writing? I asked myself. But on seeing his hopeful expression and hearing his eager pleas, I hesitated a little and then took it.

"Go home, Liang."

He looked up and gazed into the distance towards the far end of the river: "The boat isn't here yet." He stood stubbornly and refused to leave.

Liang was in bad shape. I thought it was perhaps because he had stayed up for many nights trying to finish writing his novel. He looked frail and weak and had lost a lot of weight. The clothes he wore were too thin for the harsh winter weather; his body was shaking and his teeth were chattering with cold ...

I couldn't help but think of the scene many years ago: on the snowy field, a naked boy frolicking in the snow ... *Where is that Liang? Where is that Liang who was once so simple,*

157

pure and innocent? The boat arrived. I untied my scarf and wrapped it around his neck. He didn't move, and it felt as if I were tying it around the trunk of a dying tree. I hurried to the boat. I waved to him, but he didn't wave back. The ship left the dock, and as I looked at him I thought how beautiful he still was.

The boat rounded a bend in the river and Liang, now hidden behind trees, disappeared from view. A moment later, the ancestral hall appeared in front of me. Standing by the river in the twilight, it looked taller and sturdier than I remembered. I didn't know just how many years of wind and rain the hall had endured, but it seemed to be as impressive as ever ...

Peking University, October 1984

This book is the result of a co-publication agreement between Guangdong Education Publishing House Co., Ltd.(China) and Paths International Ltd (UK)

Title: The Red Tiles: Tales from China
Author: Cao Wenxuan
Translated by Huaicun Zhang
Hardback ISBN: 978-1-84464-597-8
Paperback ISBN: 978-1-84464-599-2
Ebook ISBN: 978-1-84464-598-5

Paths International Ltd
www.pathsinternational.com

Published in United Kingdom

CPSIA information can be obtained
at www.ICGtesting.com
Printed in the USA
LVHW050727080121
675928LV00005B/59/J